Fugitive is Catherin[...]
Her previous books are *Run, Zan, Run*, which won the Kathleen Fidler Award and more recently the Verghereto Award in Italy, and *Fighting Back*. She also writes comedy, and has had two situation comedy series on BBC Radio 2. Catherine lives in Greenock with her family, where she indulges her lifelong love of writing.

Some other books by Catherine MacPhail

FIGHTING BACK
RUN, ZAN, RUN

Fugitive

Catherine MacPhail

PUFFIN BOOKS

For Iain and Irene

PUFFIN BOOKS

Published by the Penguin Group
Penguin Books Ltd, 27 Wrights Lane, London w8 5tz, England
Penguin Putnam Inc., 375 Hudson Street, New York, New York 10014, USA
Penguin Books Australia Ltd, Ringwood, Victoria, Australia
Penguin Books Canada Ltd, 10 Alcorn Avenue, Toronto, Ontario, Canada m4v 3b2
Penguin Books (NZ) Ltd, Private Bag 102902, NSMC, Auckland, New Zealand

Penguin Books Ltd, Registered Offices: Harmondsworth, Middlesex, England

First published 1999
4

Set in 12/14pt Monotype Baskerville
Typeset by Rowland Phototypesetting Ltd,
Bury St Edmunds, Suffolk
Made and printed in England by Clays Ltd, St Ives plc

British Library Cataloguing in Publication Data
A CIP catalogue record for this book is available from the British Library

isbn 0-140-38271-2

I

'*O*K, what age am I tonight, Mother?'

Jack leaned back in his seat, enjoying the ride in spite of his mother's driving. He watched in amusement as she tried to get the windscreen wipers to work, and only succeeded in flashing her lights at other drivers.

'Goodness, don't you think you should find out how the car works before you get a loan of it?' he said. He flicked a switch and the windscreen wipers came on immediately. He sat back again, smug. 'The police will be stopping us any minute, thinking you've stolen it.'

'Oh, belt up!' his mother, Big Rose, said, blowing a strand of fair hair back from her face.

'Charming way to talk to your wee boy,' Jack said. He seldom called her Big Rose to her face. She might really have belted him if he did. He added with a grin, 'By the way, it's stopped raining.'

His mother scowled at him. 'One more word from you and you're walking.'

Jack shut up. He knew she didn't mean it, but he also knew she'd had enough for one night. First she hadn't been able to release the steering lock on the car, then she had reversed over the wheely bin on the pavement, and finally she had inadvertently opened the sun roof just when it had begun to pour.

'Stupid car!' she said for the hundredth time.

It had been Alec Shepherd in her office who had offered her the car (and his new one at that) for the evening. He had probably included himself in the offer. She had turned him down, as she turned down every man who was interested in her.

'My little boy is the only man in my life,' she would say, hopefully out of earshot of any of his friends, and she would ruffle his hair and he hated it when she did that.

She had not turned down the car however. She seldom did. They both loved films, and since the nearest cinema was across the river the only way to get there was by car. So once a month she took Alec up on his offer and they'd drive over the bridge to see the latest film. However, since this was Alec's new car, it might have helped if she'd found out how it worked first.

He was silent for another few minutes. Finally he asked again, 'Can I just ask what age I am tonight?'

She turned her eyes back to the road. 'You know I won't know till we get there.'

It was a standing joke that Jack's age changed depending on the film they were going to see. He was, officially, thirteen. But for a twelve film – and a half-price ticket – he looked as small and innocent as he could to get in. The small wasn't difficult. He was small even for thirteen, which made trying to look fifteen – when he had to – even more difficult.

Tonight was a fifteen. Sylvester Stallone. All action for him. All rippling muscles for his mum.

He stayed in the background while she bought the tickets. No questions asked. The trouble came from the man who took their tickets as they were going into the hall. He looked Jack up and down, and then up again.

'He's never fifteen,' he said.

His mother hesitated; ran her tongue over her lips. 'What?' she asked.

The man began shaking his head cockily. 'I said, that WEE boy –' Jack could almost see the capital letters come out of his mouth – 'is never fifteen.'

'Of course he is!' his mother snapped, dragging Jack protectively towards her.

The man was not taking that at all. 'Have you got his birth certificate with you?'

His mother almost flew at him. 'No. I do not have his birth certificate with me. We're going to the pictures. We're not leaving the country.'

The man continued to shake his head. 'I'm afraid I can't –'

He didn't get another word out. His mother leapt forward like a tigress. 'Well, thank you very much! Do you know that boy of mine has a complex about his height? I've had him in therapy to help him get over it. This is practically the first time I've been able to take him out in public!'

Jack watched the man's face grow redder and redder. He was trying to get a word in. No change with Big Rose.

'And we have to come across someone as insensitive as you!' Big Rose pulled Jack even closer and sniffed. Jack tried to keep his face straight.

The man began to blurt out. 'Look, I'm sorry ... I didn't know ... I didn't understand.' He was already releasing the cord to let them past. 'My apologies. Honest.'

His mother sniffed again. What an actress! 'Just let us in, please.'

'Of course. Of course.' And as he moved aside his mother swept regally past him, dragging Jack behind her.

'You're brilliant, Mother!' Jack whispered.

'And how often have I told you to slink inside when you're supposed to be fifteen. But not Jack! You saunter up, hands in your pockets. No wonder he noticed you!'

'I just forgot,' Jack said.

4

There was a sudden commotion behind them. 'Hold on there!'

Jack swallowed. He recognized the voice. It was the man again. Jack froze to the spot. 'Hold on there!'

His mother held his hand tightly. He would never allow her to do that under normal circumstances, but if he was going to be thrown out of the cinema he was going to make sure she was coming too. They both turned slowly. The man was hurrying toward them.

'Here, son.' He suddenly pressed something into Jack's hand. It was a Mars bar. 'And don't you worry. I was wee when I was a boy,' he laughed. 'But you grow out of it.'

And he turned and hurried away. All one and a half metres of him.

Sylvester Stallone was great. It was a brilliant film. All the way home in the car, Jack was the hero. Fighting off villains, climbing rock faces, dangling from cliffs. He wouldn't have bothered rescuing the (so-called) beautiful heroine though. He would have let her drop. She was a real drip anyway. But for everything else the film was perfect. It had adventure and excitement – all the things that never happened in his life. His life was so boring.

It was his mother who made his life interesting,

he had to admit. It was a laugh a minute with Big Rose. He glanced at her now as she drove home, intent on the road ahead. He wondered if she too was dreaming of an adventure. Or was she quite content – Just her and Jack and an occasional visit to the cinema in a borrowed car?

2

'So, what did Big Rose do then?' Jack had a group of his pals gathered around him. They had been listening intently as he regaled them with the latest adventures of Big Rose. He exaggerated a little. He always did. But he didn't have to exaggerate very much where his mother was concerned. He had just told them that she had a stranglehold on the man at the pictures and his face was turning blue as she told him about her poor 'wee son'.

'So go on, what did she do then?' his best friend, Sandy, asked, eager for the rest of the story.

Jack hesitated. He knew the old saying well. Make 'em laugh, make 'em cry, make 'em wait. That was his motto when it came to telling stories.

'She dropped him like a hot kebab, and he

collapsed on the carpet. Then she wiped her hands together, looked at me and said, "OK, kid. Come on. The coast is clear." '

He finished up with the tale about the Mars bar. They loved that.

'Honest, Jack,' Sandy said, 'I could listen to you talking about your mum all day.'

Sandy was a great friend to have. He liked to listen, which suited Jack very well – he loved to talk.

The story pleased the rest of them too. They all laughed, except for Joe Grady who stood at the far corner of the playground and scowled at him.

'What a load of baloney,' he said.

'You don't believe me, Grady?' Jack fished in his pocket. 'You want proof?' He took something and flung it at him. 'The very Mars bar. I didn't finish it – you can eat the rest. It's kinda hairy 'cause it's been in my pocket all weekend.'

They all laughed again and Joe Grady squashed the Mars bar under his foot.

'You talk a load of rubbish, Jack Tarrant!' Joe sneered. 'Of course, my mother says that's because you're with your mother all the time. You're just a mummy's boy.'

Joe knew well how to needle him. Jack felt his ears go red.

'You're always listening to gossip and passing

on gossip, just like a wee woman – just like your mother.'

Jack wanted desperately to fly at him. He thought of Sylvester Stallone and the flying leap he had made at the villain on Saturday night. Should he risk trying it? He decided against it. Sylvester Stallone had probably practised a lot and then used a stunt man. And anyway, that was never how Jack handled things. He made a joke of it all the time. He did now.

'My mother isn't a wee woman. My mother's the creature in *Alien*. She eats guys like you for her dinner.'

It worked as it always did. Everyone laughed and Joe Grady shrugged and moved off with his friends.

But it did hurt Jack. How it hurt. Just because it *was* always him and his mother. Always had been. He could hardly remember his dad – a vague figure who had died when Jack was only three. His mother had moved here, to this town, shortly after that, got her job in the estate agent's office, bought their house. Oh, and he loved that house – two bedrooms upstairs and a big, empty, warm cellar he had always played in. Since then it had just been him and his mum. It had never bothered Jack. He enjoyed life with her in fact – until recently. Until he'd come to the high school and met Joe Grady.

'Why hasn't your mother got a boyfriend?'

He was asked that often. Lots of his pals didn't have a dad, but there was usually a man somewhere in their life.

'Big Rose terrifies them,' he would always answer, and everyone would laugh. Everyone except Joe.

'Maybe she's too ugly, if she looks anything like you,' he would sneer at him.

And Jack would always joke back with him. 'And you obviously take after your father. What was his name again? King Kong?'

But it wasn't just Joe who hurt him. His teachers did too, even the nice ones. Especially the nice ones, who worried about him. Miss Rodgers from Maths for instance.

'I really feel you need a male role model, Jack,' she had said once. 'It's very important at your age.'

Jack had just smiled. What on earth was a role model? he wondered.

Miss Rodgers told him with her next breath. 'A man in your life. You have no father, or brothers or uncles. Not even a grandfather. Have you?' She tutted and looked worried again, and Jack had smiled once again to hide the hurt.

He sometimes wondered too why his mother had never had a boyfriend. She certainly wasn't ugly. In fact he'd heard her being described as a 'fine figure of a woman.' But that had been by Mr Gallacher at the bottom of the road who was half blind and thought the local grocer was Adolf Hitler in disguise. (It must have been a really good disguise – the grocer was a Pakistani.) However, it had to be admitted that Big Rose was a nice-looking woman. She had fair hair like Jack's, and it was always cut into a very chic style. She was always very fashionably dressed, usually in short skirts. (A bit too short in Jack's opinion, but she seemed to think she had nice legs.) And it wasn't as if she didn't like men. He had caught her drooling (yes, drooling) in front of the television whenever her favourite actors were on.

Yet, as far as he could remember, there had never been a boyfriend. Not even a date. Alec from the office was the nearest thing she'd ever had to a boyfriend, and he was sure the only reason she was nice to him was because he lent her the car.

He sometimes wondered about it as he lay in bed at night. Was she still crazy about his dad? Couldn't get over him? She never talked about his dad, and didn't have a photo of him anywhere. Jack had long since stopped asking questions about him that were never answered anyway. It was too painful for her, he thought.

No, the final conclusion he always came to was

that men were indeed terrified of Big Rose. She wasn't exactly your damsel-in-distress type. There wasn't a dragon this side of heaven that would be able to get near her, let alone eat her up.

So it was a complete surprise to him that night when he came home from school and found Alec Shepherd had been invited to tea.

3

'So, I believe you're a footballer?'

They had finished tea and his mother was upstairs getting ready for her date.

Her date? Jack still couldn't get over it.

'A goalkeeper,' he corrected. Alec wasn't a bad-looking guy. He smiled a lot, probably because he had very white, even teeth. Jack wondered if they were real.

'Play in the school team, don't you?'

Jack nodded.

'How are you doing in the league?'

'We're at the bottom,' Jack confessed. 'We're rubbish.'

Alec laughed. 'Well, you're honest.'

'I am to goalkeeping what Arnold Schwarzenegger is to ballet dancing.'

Alec laughed again. Goodness, he was easy to amuse.

'You get that sense of humour from your mother,' Alec said.

'Probably.'

Alec pretended he was studying the tablecloth. 'She's a very nice lady.'

'I like her,' Jack said.

He could tell Alec was having a problem finding anything else to say. Jack enjoyed his discomfort. He blew chewing gum and stared at Alec till his mother came downstairs. Alec was on his feet like a shot.

'What are you all dressed up for?' Jack asked. His mother was wearing a slinky black suit and her best pearls. 'I thought you were only going for a coffee.'

'We might go somewhere nice.' His mother threw her answer back at him.' I am allowed to get dressed up now and then, I suppose?'

'Put on a hat and you could go to a wedding,' he told her. She threw his anorak at him.

'I'll pick you up on the way home.'

'Why? Where am I going?' He had intended staying in. There was an all-action movie on television tonight.

'I've arranged for you to go to Mrs Ferriers.'

'No way! I'd rather sleep on a bed of nails,' he said.

His mother was not moved. 'Any more of your cheek and that can be arranged.'

Mrs Ferrier was a sort of friend of his mother. She was all right – it was her daughter Jack objected to. Lizzie Ferrier was in Jack's class at school. She was in the same boat as Jack, almost. Her father had died two years before, but any sympathy Jack might have had was lost because she was so obnoxious. Joe Grady considered Lizzie Ferrier his girlfriend. Jack thought they were well matched – one was as bad as the other. He hoped she wasn't in. His wish was not granted.

'Lizzie's up in her room, Jack,' Mrs Ferrier told him as soon as he arrived. 'Go on up, dear.'

Lizzie was lying face down on the bed flicking over the pages of a book lying on the floor. 'Oh, I didn't know I was babysitting tonight,' she said with a sneer as he came in.

'I don't need a babysitter. I just thought I'd bring you some spot-removing cream.'

That got to her. He could always get to her by mentioning her spots. She sat up cross-legged on the bed. 'And I believe your mother's actually got a DATE!'

He resented her sounding so surprised, even though that had been his reaction too. 'It's not really a date.' He thought for a moment. 'It's a works outing.'

'Still,' Lizzie said, 'it's the first time she's gone

13

on a . . .' There was a long pause. She could be so theatrical. 'Works outing. Is he nice?'

Typical female question. 'Oh, he's gorgeous,' he simpered.

Lizzie was quiet for a moment. If only he could talk to her the way he could talk to his mother or to his mates, but it was impossible. It was always as if she was thinking up some devious plan to embarrass him.

'Why do you think she's never gone out on a date before?'

Did everybody wonder about his mother and her manless state? he wondered.

'She's never found anybody to live up to my standards,' he said. 'Anyway, how would you feel if your mother went out on a date?'

She shrugged that away. 'My dad's only been dead two years. How long has yours been dead?'

'I can't even remember him,' he said.

'You don't get much of a chance, do you?' Lizzie said smugly. 'You don't even have a picture of him in your house.' She lifted the picture of her dad from her bedside table. There were pictures of him all over their house; a dark-eyed smiling man with a mane of dark hair. Lizzie looked a lot like him . . . except for the smile. 'Why is that, Jack?'

Lizzie always asked difficult questions. Why was that indeed?

He asked his mother later when they were back home and Alec had gone.

'I've told you before. I haven't got any,' she said at once, very casually, not looking at him. 'He wasn't one for having his picture taken.'

'Didn't you have any wedding pictures taken?'

'I lost them when we moved. What is this, the third degree? What brought this on?'

He was a little afraid to tell her. How would Big Rose take it?

'People keep asking about my dad. And Mrs Rodgers says I need a role model.'

She nearly jumped a metre in the air. 'A what?'

'A role model,' he began to explain. 'A man I can look up to and admire and copy.'

'Stick a poster of Nelson Mandela above your bed then.'

'Well, maybe if you told me something about my dad. I don't know anything about him. Whenever I ask, you change the subject.'

'There's nothing to tell, Jack.' She said it quickly. 'He was only in your life for three years, and now he's dead.' She hesitated. 'He was a nice man. He was a . . .' She seemed to be thinking about what to say next. 'What is there to say? He took sick. He died. OK? Now, you need a role model, like I need a man in my life – not at all!'

4

*Y*et maybe his words had sunk in because in the next three months Alec appeared quite a lot. He had Sunday dinner with them. He took them bowling, and once he even came to the pictures with them.

'What age am I tonight?' Jack had asked mischievously.

His mother's nudge had almost sent him flying into an Indian takeaway. 'Your own age, of course.'

He had to think about that for a bit. 'What age is that again?'

Alec seemed to enjoy these outings. He seemed to like Big Rose. Amazingly, he seemed to like Jack as well. And one Sunday afternoon, he even appeared at the school football match. Jack was never so glad to see anyone in his life. His mother usually came on her own and embarrassed the life out of him – harrassing the referee, screaming abuse at the other team. Once, she even had to be ordered off the pitch when she scrummed an oversize forward who'd been picking on Jack.

Alec was much quieter. Waving a greeting to him as he came on to the pitch, clapping and shouting encouragement to him along with the other fathers . . .

The other fathers.

That even sounded funny thinking about it. Jack actually wanted to show off, make Alec proud of him, impress him.

Unfortunately, they lost again. Eight–nil.

'Never mind,' Alec said, as he took him home. 'You'll do better next time.'

Dinner was ready when they got back. A cold February afternoon, and Mother with a big roast dinner waiting for the men coming home. It could almost have been an Oxo advert. Was this how families felt? He liked it, he decided.

'How did you do?' his mother asked. Then, before he could answer, she said, 'Don't tell me, how much did you lose by this time?'

Jack shrugged and took his seat at the table. 'Wasn't too bad. Only eight-nil.'

'Oh well,' she grinned, 'you're getting better.'

Alec still didn't catch on with their humour, didn't understand how they could insult each other like this.

'But tell her, Jack.' He smiled up at Big Rose. 'Jack was voted Man of the Match by his team.'

If he expected that to impress his mother, he still didn't know her very well. She went into a fit of the giggles. Alec looked hurt for Jack.

'He was Man of the Match?' his mother managed to say in between giggles. 'Best player on the team?'

Jack nodded and started eating his roast beef.

'And your team lost eight–nil?'

Jack nodded again.

'And you're the goalkeeper?'

Now she was almost in hysterics. Jack looked at Alec and shrugged his shoulders. Alec looked embarrassed.

'The rest of the team must be really bad!'

'Do you see what I've got to put up with, Alec?' Jack asked him. 'Who would have a mother like that?'

'My son. Man of the Match.' She sat down, shaking her head, still giggling.

Alec was watching her, puzzled. Finally, he gave up. 'I'll never understand you two.'

Later, his mother came up and sat on his bed. 'Well, did you like Alec coming to the match?'

'Yes.' He paused. 'That's why we did so well, I was trying to impress him.' She threw back her head and laughed. So did Jack.

'Are you two getting serious?'

'No.' She answered at once. 'Don't even think

about it. He's a nice man, and I like him. But it ends there. Right?'

But did it? Jack, for once in his life, wasn't sure about his mother's feelings. Did she kiss Alec? And if she did, surely that meant she more than liked him. He liked Miss Potts, the French teacher, but she had hair coming out of her nose and a moustache. The thought of kissing her made him want to throw up. No, he decided. If he caught his mother kissing Alec, then there was a good chance he was going to have a regular supporter at his football matches.

He settled down that night thinking maybe having another man in the house wouldn't be so bad after all.

5

*L*izzie Ferrier was getting spottier, Jack decided. He couldn't take his eyes off her all through Maths.

'Hey, you keep your eyes off my bird.' Joe Grady nudged him as he came out of the class. 'I saw you watching her.'

Jack shrugged. 'I couldn't help it. She's got such an interesting face.'

Lizzie fluttered her eyelashes and simpered.

'I mean,' Jack went on, 'I thought skin like that went out of fashion with the Black Death.'

The crowd around him roared with laughter. Only Lizzie Ferrier didn't laugh. her big eyes widened and seemed to fill up. Was she hurt?

For a minute he felt guilty. No. Make that thirty seconds. For suddenly those same eyes flashed with venom. 'At least I get something for my spots. I hope you can get something for your black eye!'

Stupid girl. 'What black eye?' Jack asked, as if he was talking to an idiot.

'This one,' Joe Grady sneered.

Jack didn't see it coming. He didn't expect it. Joe's fist right in his face.

It sent him staggering backwards against the wall. He saw stars, he really did. He'd always thought that only happened in cartoons. By the time he'd realized what was happening, Joe Grady, knight in shining armour, had left with his own little dragon, Lizzie.

Sandy helped him to his feet. 'That's going to be a cracker.' He peered at Jack's eye with something like admiration; envy even. 'Joe's some fighter, isn't he?'

Jack blinked a few times to try to get Sandy's face – both of them – into focus. 'He took me by surprise. He fights dirty. I could beat him any day in a fair fight.'

Sandy shook his head. 'Naw,' he said, 'you're nearly as good a fighter as you are a goalie.' He laughed. 'You're rubbish.'

They went off down the corridor to their next class arguing. 'Are you supposed to be my best friend?' Jack asked him.

'That's why I can tell you the truth. Pick on somebody else's girlfriend. Gary O'Hagan's only half your size. You could beat him easy. Pick on his girlfriend.'

Jack was affronted. 'I don't pick on people. I'm a nice boy. Joe Grady picks on me. And that Lizzie Ferrier's nasty.'

Sandy studied him for a minute. 'You sure you don't fancy her? I saw you watching her as well, you know.'

Jack stuck two fingers down his throat and pretended to be sick. 'She's ugly. Have you never noticed that, Sandy? I'd never be that desperate for a girlfriend.'

By four o'clock his eye was black and swollen. He told his teachers that he had walked into a door. Nobody seemed to believe him. He had the same story ready for his mother. She wouldn't believe it either.

'Get your mother to put a big juicy steak on it. It really does work,' Miss Potts suggested helpfully.

He could just hear his mother if he suggested a big juicy steak for his eye. She was a one-parent family, she would say. She reminded him of this on a regular basis. He'd be lucky if she put an economy hamburger on his eye – and then she would probably stick it in a roll and expect him to eat it afterwards.

They had auditions for the school show that day, so by the time he came home his mother was already there. He could hear her in the living room. The news had just finished, so she'd be settling down to watch one of those awful Australian soaps that she loved.

He prepared himself and his eye with his story and stepped into the room. 'Hello, Mum,' he began. She turned suddenly as if she hadn't been expecting him. Her face was white. She looked as if she'd begun to cry. 'Are you all right, Mum?' She stood up and switched off the television.

Switched off the television? Just as her favourite programme had started? Something was definitely wrong.

'I'm fine,' she lied. Jack new she lied. She wasn't fine. She hardly looked at him; still hadn't noticed his eye. 'I'll get your tea.'

She brushed past him into the kitchen. He watched her through the crack in the door. Watched as she clenched her fists and pushed them against her mouth, listened as she murmured with a sob, 'Please no. Don't let it be true. Not that . . . please!'

6

*B*ig Rose insisted nothing was wrong and kept insisting even when he went to bed.

Jack lay for a long time, thinking about it. Could it be Alec? Had they fallen out? If it had upset her this much she must be really in love with him, despite what she was always saying.

Or had she found out she had some terrible illness? That thought brought Jack out in a cold sweat. His mother ill? He'd never known her to be ill. Not Big Rose.

And if anything happened to her . . . What would happen to him? He had no family. No grandparents either side, no cousins, no aunts or uncles. He would be completely alone if . . .

He blotted that awful, unthinkable thought out. His mother would be fine, he decided. She's probably been upset at the death of a favourite character from one of those daft soaps. Yes, that would be it.

Still, he didn't sleep well that night, dreaming of giant birds flapping around him, their great black wings blotting out the light, while he tried to fight them off with a feather.

In the morning, she seemed better. Things were always better in the morning.

'Everything OK, Mum?' he had asked.

'A-one OK!' had been her reply, as she tried to scrape his burnt toast discreetly into the sink. 'We'll have to get something for that eye tonight.'

'Miss Potts suggested a sirloin steak,' he informed her.

'Miss Potts can supply it then. I was thinking more of a cold cloth.'

His eye was a talking point at school. People actually came up to him and asked to examine it. By the afternoon he was considering charging them.

'That's a cracker!' they would say. 'Joe Grady's got some punch, hasn't he?'

As for Spotty Lizzie, she was mincing about with her nose in the air as if she was something.

'Everybody thinks you and Joe were fighting over her,' Sandy said.

'I wasn't fighting!' Jack reminded him, saying it loud enough so anyone else in the vicinity could hear. 'I was getting punched.'

Mad Marshall, the music teacher, appeared in the afternoon and asked those who'd auditioned for the school show the day before to join him in the hall during break.

'During break!' Jack mouthed to Sandy. 'Is he kidding? I'm not that keen for a part.'

They went anyway, filing in with the rest of them to hear if their names were called. Jack expected to be in the chorus, like last year when he'd been a Russian peasant in *Fiddler on the Roof*.

Mad informed them right away that this year's musical was going to be *Calamity Jane*.

'I think you're going to have a lot of fun doing it,' he informed them proudly. 'The songs are good and there's a lot of humour in it.' He then treated them to one of the songs he was sure they'd enjoy singing. 'The Deadwood Stage' was rolling out all over the school hall.

Everyone just glanced at each other. Mad Marshall was at it again, living up to his well-earned nickname. He finished his song and beamed at everyone. No one knew whether to clap or not. 'We are going to have *such* fun with this one.' It was an order not a suggestion.

To Jack's astonishment, he gave the main part, your actual Calamity Jane, to Lizzie Ferrier. He wasn't the only one who was astonished. Lily Meldrum, who was used to playing the lead in the school shows, burst into tears. Girls! What would you do with them!

Jack tugged at her elbow. 'Calamity Jane's supposed to be ugly. The part was written for Lizzie.'

This didn't stem Lily's tears. She still had to be comforted by her friends.

'Now, now, Lily. You've got a wonderful part. You're playing Katie Brown, Calamity's best friend. And all the men in town are after her.'

This brightened Lily just a little.

Jack couldn't see Lizzie, but he could imagine her beaming from ear to ear, her spots bursting with pride, probably splashing everyone who was in front of her. The thought made him giggle. The other top roles were allocated and Jack whispered to Sandy, 'Looks like you and me in the chorus again. Cowboys!' They began firing imaginary guns.

'Jack! Jack Tarrant, are you here?'

Jack pushed forward so Mad could see him. 'Who? Me, sir?'

'I was most impressed with your audition, and how funny you were last year.'

Jack threw a puzzled glance at Sandy. Had he been funny last year?

'So, you can be the comic relief this year. You're going to play Francis Fryer. Oh, it's a great part. Lots of laughs.'

Lily turned to him and smiled. 'Congratulations,' she said. She'd never deigned to speak a word to him before, but now that he was a star she noticed him.

Football practice was cancelled because of the

heavy rain, and Jack began to walk home. He could hardly wait to tell his mother. This would cheer her up, although he imagined she'd forgotten already whatever it was that was bothering her last night.

There was a sudden crack of thunder and a bolt of lightning. People rushed everywhere, or huddled in doorways out of the deluge. Jack decided to get the next bus. No point in coming down with pneumonia just when he was about to become a star! He rushed round the corner to the bus stop and almost knocked a man off his feet. The man swore and held him by the shoulders. He looked like a real hard man, his face grim. Jack was ready to apologize until he saw to his astonishment that the man also had the beginnings of a cracker of a black eye! The coincidence made Jack laugh. He pointed to his own eye and joked, 'Aye! Aye!'

The man didn't smile back. He obviously had no sense of humour. He pushed Jack away and hurried off down the empty street, pulling up the collar of his long black coat.

As he waited for the bus, Jack wondered how the man had got his black eye. Had he been in a fight, or had he, like Jack, just been on the wrong end of a fist? Maybe the man was wondering about Jack too. No, he looked too miserable for that. Why didn't people laugh more often? Jack thought. People took things too seriously, like a black eye, or a bit of rain. Everybody seemed to look miserable in the rain. But not Jack. He was in a great mood.

The bus went along the main road, past the police station. And that was how he came to see her – his mother, walking inside, pale-faced, between two uniformed officers.

7

*H*e sat waiting for her, wondering. What was his mother doing at the police station? It looked as if she was being arrested. But what had she done?

Shoplifting!

She was always wandering about shops putting things in her hand, not putting them into the basket in case there was a special offer – three for the price of two or something – in another aisle. He was forever telling her they were being watched. Cameras everywhere.

'Let them watch!' she would say, and lift something else and shove it under her arm.

Yes. Shoplifting. That was it, he decided.

Yet, what was his mother doing in the

supermarket on a Wednesday? She worked all day.

So if it wasn't shoplifting . . .

Maybe she had refused to pay her council tax. She was always threatening to do that.

Big Rose a jailbird. He saw her suddenly, wearing a suit with arrows. She'd probably insist on a short skirt knowing his mum.

The picture faded, melted away like one drawn on a steamy window.

No, there wasn't a jail that could hold her.

He heard the key turn in the lock at her usual time, five-thirty, and he rushed from his bedroom to see if she was alone.

'What are you doing home?' she asked, 'I thought you had football practice.'

'It's raining,' he said. Actually, there was a thunderstorm outside.

His mother pulled off her coat and shook her umbrella out on the step.

'You're letting a wee bit of rain stop you practising? No wonder Scotland never wins the World Cup.'

A crack of thunder just then seemed to be reminding her it wasn't just a 'wee bit of rain'. She ignored it. 'Anyway, you know I don't like you in the house by yourself. You should have gone to Mrs Ferriers.'

He curled his lip in disgust.

'Oh, I know, she can be a pain. But I know you like Lizzie.'

Big Rose knew exactly how he liked Lizzie. She threw back her head and laughed.

His mum was in a much better mood tonight. Maybe she hadn't been arrested after all. Maybe she'd won those two policemen in a raffle. That would put her in a good mood, winning two men in uniform.

He waited for her to tell him exactly what had happened.

And waited.

They had finished their tea and all she'd told him about was the paltry rise her boss was offering her and the drunk who'd come into the office that morning and refused to leave till the bingo next door had started.

'Eventually,' she went on, 'we had to get Tom, from the butcher's next door, to carry him out over his shoulder like a carcass of beef.' She broke into a fit of the giggles remembering the scene.

Jack drummed his fingers on the table. 'You didn't have to call the police for him or anything?'

'No. He was only a wee drunk man. Anyway, who needs the police when you've got a six foot butcher in the next shop?'

'Didn't Alec do his knight-in-shining-armour bit then?'

'He's away on a course if you must know. Won't be back till next week.'

So that explained Alec's absence over the past few days.

She stood up and took the dishes to the sink.

'So,' he went on, 'absolutely no need to inform the police then?'

'No need at all,' she answered, rinsing the cups under the tap.

He watched her closely before he spoke again. 'So, no particular need for you to have to visit the police station?'

He saw her back straighten, her head come up. He had taken her by surprise.

'What do you mean by that?'

He decided to play it like a policeman. 'Would you like to accompany both of us to the station, madam, the time is three forty-five.'

'You saw me.'

'I was on the bus.'

There was a long pause. Why did he have the feeling she was thinking up a story. 'The boss had a fine to pay, asked me to go along and pay it for him.'

'With a police escort? Must have been a big fine.'

She turned from the sink. 'I just happened to be walking in with two policemen. OK? What's the big deal? Of course, I didn't know Sherlock blinking Holmes was going to be on the case.'

She stormed out. She wasn't angry – he'd seldom seen his mother angry – but she was definitely ruffled.

She sat in the living room, watching the television, but Jack could see her mind wasn't on the prime minister's visit to the U.S. or the armed robber still on the run from prison, or even the assault on an elderly woman in the town that day. In fact, she switched the television off as soon as he joined her.

'Gloom and Doom!' she said and repeated it. 'Gloom and Doom. That's all we get on TV.'

He threw himself on the couch beside her, determined to cheer her up again. 'I've got good news.'

She grinned. 'The school's sending you away on a five-year trip, all expenses paid. You've made my day.'

'Ha! Ha! Are you going to listen, or aren't you?'

She nodded and zipped her lip and he told her about his elevation to stardom in the school musical.

'*Calamity Jane!*' she yelled. 'That's my favourite.' She then proceeded to launch herself into 'The Deadwood Stage'. What was it about that song that sent adults insane? He managed to shut her up after the first chorus.

'Mad Marshall says I'll get a few laughs in this part. I'm the comic relief, he told me.'

'Oh, you will. Especially when you dress up as a woman and sing. You see,' she went on, oblivious to his open mouth, 'all those cowboys expect Francis to be a woman so, not wanting to disappoint them, the boss makes Francis put on a frock and sing. And he nearly fools them too.' She was laughing at the thought of it. 'Until his wig gets caught in the trombone and starts going in and out with the music. Then there's a riot. Oh, it'll be hilarious.'

Jack listened in mounting horror. 'I'm supposed to wear a frock?'

'Of course.' She began to explain the reasons to him. He wouldn't listen.

'This is a show with cowboys and Indians — and I'm the idiot that's supposed to put on a frock?'

'Just for this one song.'

He was shaking his head. 'No way! I get called mummy's boy enough at that school without dressing up as a girl!'

He would tell Mad Marshall tomorrow. There was no way he was going to play Francis Fryer.

He stood at the window in his bedroom watching the dark street. A car was revving its engine in the distance, but apart from that and the rain, the night was silent.

Then it appeared, so quietly he thought the engine was off and it was freewheeling down the street.

A police car. It slowed as it came to their house and one of the policemen turned towards their door and stared. Then, just as silently, it moved off.

A police car ... showing such an interest in their house?

Something was going on. He was sure of it. But what?

8

'*B*ut this is ridiculous, Jack! It's a great part!' Mad Marshall was mad. 'I thought you liked making people laugh.'

Jack scuffed his toe against a chair. 'I do. I just don't like them laughing *at* me.'

Mad watched him as if he was totally puzzled by that statement. Then he shook his head. 'I don't understand you, Jack. There's only one scene when you wear a dress.'

How could he explain it to him? How could he explain it to anyone?

'I'm not wearing a dress,' he insisted.

'If I remember rightly,' Mad said, 'you wore a dress at last year's Hallowe'en party.'

'I was younger then,' Jack said.

He hadn't even thought about it then. He had enjoyed himself thoroughly until Lizzie had begun picking on him.

'That you in your mummy's dress?' she had taunted, making sure everyone heard and saw his embarrassment. 'Aren't you pretty? Mummy's boy!'

Mummy's boy!

The words had rung in his ear for a long time. Mummy's boy.

Mad finally saw that all his coaxing was to no avail. He shook his head. 'You're back in the chorus then.'

Jack shrugged. 'Suits me.'

'Will you at least understudy the part?'

Jack looked blank and Mad explained what he meant. 'Learn the part. Help the boy who will play Francis?'

'Sure, who is that?'

Mad checked down his list. 'Angus Paige,' he said with a sigh.

Angus, Jack decided as he went off to his class, would make an excellent substitute. He was the tallest boy in the school, and always walked with a stoop in the hope that no one would notice him. His voice hadn't broken yet either, so he spoke in a high-pitched nasal whine. He probably sang like that too. Yes, he'd make a perfect Francis Fryer.

He informed Sandy of his decision over lunch. Sandy was delighted. 'Great! We'll be cowboys together.'

They began firing imaginary guns at each other, then throwing peas. It was when the mashed potatoes started flying around the canteen that the dinner lady intervened, grabbing them both and throwing them out.

All in all, it was a good day.

Joe Grady was caught passing a note to Lizzie Ferrier, which the teacher proceeded to read out to the whole class.

'You've got me in a tizzy, Lizzie,' it read.

What a nerd! The whole school soon heard of it and it was repeated every time Joe Grady moved into view.

What a laugh!

Lizzie was really mad. She went bright red. Even her spots blushed.

Jack's good humour stayed with him all day, even after tea when he sat in the living room, watching television. His mother was right, he thought. Gloom and doom.

The escaped armed robber's face stared at him threateningly from the screen, then the story switched to the old woman, still unconscious after the vicious assault.

He was in too good a mood to watch that for long. He switched off the television and lifted the phone. He'd phone Sandy.

His mother was already on the phone. He could hear her voice, softly on the line. 'You'll make sure of that, won't you?' she sounded worried, and he was about to hang up when a man's voice answered her.

'Don't worry, Mrs Tarrant. We're keeping an eye on the house. You're safe. You're both safe.'

Jack listened, baffled. Then his mother spoke again and Jack had never heard such fear in her voice. 'I've kept this secret for so long, inspector. Promise me no one will ever find out.'

9

What was his mother doing talking to an inspector? A police inspector? Of course it was a police inspector. Jack knew that without even thinking about it.

What was going on? They were keeping an eye on the house. Well, he had seen that. But why?

Were they in danger? And from what? She'd been keeping a secret. From him?

He wanted desperately to ask her when she came downstairs to make supper, But she was so casual, so ordinary – joking with him, laughing, making him laugh – that he began to think he'd imagined that call. Perhaps it hadn't been her voice on the phone, perhaps somehow a crossed line had connected him with some other mysterious phone call.

'That can happen,' Sandy assured him, when Jack had told him about it next day. He had to tell someone or he would have burst. 'I saw it in a film on television. A woman heard people planning a murder and it turned out they were going to murder her!'

'But this isn't a film. This is real life.'

Sandy thought about that for a while. Then he poked him in the ribs. 'Hey, Jack, maybe this is an adventure!'

He'd always wanted an adventure. And how would Arnold Schwarzenegger or Sylvester Stallone deal with this one? Somehow he couldn't imagine them overhearing their mother on the phone. No. It would be a girlfriend, or an FBI agent. What would they do? Well, they'd be on their guard for a start. Watching for everything. Looking for clues. That's what Jack was going to do. He was going to get to the bottom of this mystery.

Mystery. He liked that word. He'd always wanted a mystery in his life. Now maybe he had one.

Rehearsals began after school that day for *Calamity Jane*. He and Sandy had a ball cracking whips and jumping about all over the place till, finally, Mad had put them both on detention for it. Angus Paige was rubbish! He had a cold and kept sneezing all over the cowboys. And Lizzie Ferrier kept forgetting the words of 'The Deadwood Stage'.

She didn't have to worry, however. Mad threw himself into every part. He cracked his whip and sang until everyone forgot Lizzie was even there.

'I think, deep down, he wants to play Calamity Jane himself,' Jack whispered to Sandy.

Rehearsals were cut short when Mad threw himself off the stage in his enthusiasm.

'We're going to be wonderful!' he called after them as a couple of cowboys helped him to his feet. 'Back tomorrow!'

Lizzie Ferrier was right in front of Jack as they filed out. It was irresistible!

'At least Mad will make a better-looking Calamity Jane!'

Lizzie turned on him in a fury, trying desperately to think of something clever to throw back at him. She couldn't think of a thing.

'Don't point your zits at me, Ferrier!' he teased,

and then, pulling Sandy behind him, he was off laughing and running.

He told his mother all about it that night, all except for the things he'd said to Lizzie. Big Rose would have hit the roof about that. But she fell about laughing at his description of Mad falling off the stage halfway through his song.

He loved making his mother laugh. She made him laugh too, telling him all about her day. She usually told him everything, but she was holding something back now. He knew that. She had a secret . . .

'There's a police car passing our window,' he said to her later that night. He was ready for bed. She was preparing to watch the late-night film.

She didn't even glance up at him to answer. 'It's about time we had a police patrol in this area.'

'They were here last night too.'

She smirked. 'Of course. I wouldn't expect Sherlock Holmes to miss that. Let's hope they're here tomorrow night as well.'

She was good, his mother. She spoke so casually he could almost believe that's all there was to it. A police neighbourhood patrol. Something the area had been crying out for for years. She didn't look his way, concentrating on getting the right channel for her film.

If he could just forget that phone call and those words: 'You're safe. You're both safe.'

But safe from what?

10

*A*lec came back on Monday and on Monday night was sitting with them for his tea. It was nice seeing him again, Jack decided. Especially since he'd brought him a present.

He unwrapped it eagerly, sure it was a new computer game. Unfortunately, it was only a book.

'Your mother said you don't read enough,' Alec told him. Jack frowned at his mother. She had a mischievous look in her eye.

'I hope it's called *How to Play Football in Ten Easy Lessons*,' she laughed.

'I'm learning. I'm learning,' he defended himself, looking at Alec. 'I saved one yesterday, you know.'

'Aye,' his mother said with a giggle, 'with his head. It almost knocked him out.'

'It did not almost knock me out.'

'It gave you a nasty black eye though,' Alec peered at his eye, all concern.

'No. That was another incident entirely,' his mother said. By this time she was doubled in two laughing. 'He walked into a door, didn't you, dear?'

Jack was about to agree with that, but his mother didn't pause. 'A door with five fingers and a fist!'

She took a seat at the table with them, still laughing. Alec was looking at her baffled. 'I don't understand how you two can joke about things like that,' he said.

His mother sniffed and tried to look serious. But just for a moment she glanced at Jack. A glance that spoke volumes. Alec was nice, it seemed to say, but he could never fit in with us.

'Did you tell Alec about the school play?' she said, to change the subject. 'They're doing *Calamity Jane*, Alec.'

Alec's eyes lit up. Jack knew what was coming. Alec launched himself into 'The Deadwood Stage'.

What was it about that Deadwood Stage? The next minute, his mother had joined in. Jack stuffed a chip in each ear and folded his arms. 'This is chronic!' he shouted.

Finally, they drew the stage to a halt, breathless, laughing, reminiscing about someone called Doris Day.

'Jack could have had a star part,' his mother

informed Alec. 'He could have played Francis Fryer.'

'I'm not dressing up in a frock!' Jack said flatly.

To his surprise, Alec agreed with him. 'I don't blame him. When I was his age I wouldn't have put on a frock.'

Big Rose nudged him. 'You mean you'd put one on now?' Alec began to laugh. Big Rose laughed too. They were looking at each other in a funny way, as if they really liked each other.

Jack was glad Alec was back. After all the strange things that had been happening, Alec brought normality. He made him believe everything was going to be all right now.

They stayed in, all three of them. And that was nice too. The only problem was his mother wouldn't let Jack watch TV. She forced them all to play Scrabble instead.

'You must be the world's worst speller, Jack,' she kept telling him. 'There are two T's in battered. As you're going to find out when I b-a-T-T-er you!'

'Does that mean I get more points?'

All in all, it was a good night.

Alec left after supper. They stood at the door and watched him go in his car.

'You like him, don't you?' Big Rose said as she came in to say goodnight.

'If I say yes, does that mean you're going to marry him?'

'I've got to like him before I do that.'

'Ah,' Jack said, 'but you do, don't you?'

Was there a hint of a blush on her cheeks? Maybe not. Maybe it was just the red bulb in his dinosaur lamp.

He woke with a start, still half in a dream world of Scrabble letters and stagecoaches. The room was dark, with just a shaft of moonlight slicing its way across the floor. What had woken him? For a moment, he wasn't sure. Didn't really care either. He was too tired to care. He wanted to get back to his dream.

Suddenly, a voice was raised and he knew it wasn't the television. It wasn't some late-night movie his mother was watching. It was a man's voice. Then, his mother's answering, muted but still he could hear the anger in it.

A man's voice? In his house at this time in the morning?

Jack turned his clock to see the time. It was three a.m. What would a man be doing in his house at three in the morning?

And what man?

Alec. It could only be him, surely? His mother didn't know any other men.

Yet he had seen him go. So had he come back

44

in the quiet of the night, creeping in like a burglar so the neighbours wouldn't see him? So Jack wouldn't know?

Alec . . . staying in his house at night?

But why? He thought back to the glance his mother had thrown at him. A glance that seemed to assure him Alec was just a friend. Yet, in that same moment, he remembered the way they had been looking at each other just moments later.

But it had to be Alec. Who else did his mother know?

He'd never shared his house with anyone. He didn't think he liked the idea.

If he jumped out of bed, ran down the stairs and confronted them, Alec would go, too embarrassed to stay.

But Jack couldn't move. He lay listening to the murmured voices below, his stomach churning. He was sure he would stay awake all night now, listening. But the next thing he knew his alarm was ringing loudly beside him and the radio was suddenly switched on.

It was morning.

*H*e thought his mother looked pale at breakfast, as if she'd been awake half the night.
As if she'd been crying.

'Are you all right?' he asked her.

'Of course I am. Why shouldn't I be?'

'I thought I heard you in the middle of the
night. Talking to somebody.' He paused, watching
her closely. She didn't even glance at him. She
didn't spill the tea she was pouring. She didn't
even blush. She was good, Big Rose. 'A man,' he
finished.

'I should be so lucky,' was all she said.

'Wasn't there anybody here?'

She lifted the morning paper and began reading, avoiding his eyes. 'I couldn't sleep. I got up
and watched some T V. O K, Sherlock?'

But she was lying. He knew that.

He couldn't concentrate on his school work all
day. That wasn't unusual. He hardly ever concen-
trated on his school work. But at least today he
had an excuse.

There were more rehearsals after school and

by the time he got there he had begun to think he had imagined it all. Why would his mother lie anyway?

Forgetting about it was easy as he and Sandy watched from the sidelines as Lizzie Ferrier tried hard to look appealing while she belted out 'Once I Had a Secret Love'.

They fell about laughing all the way through until finally Lizzie stopped in the middle of shouting it from the highest hill and rushed at them. Mad Marshall almost had a canary fit.

'Children! Children! Please! Boys! You shouldn't be fighting with a defenceless little girl!'

Defenceless little girl! Lizzie had them both by the hair and was knocking their heads together like coconuts.

'Tell her to leave us be!' Jack tried to say. The rest of the cast were enjoying the proceedings enormously. Finally, it took Wild Bill Hickock as well as Mad to pull her off them.

'Detention for you boys!' Mad shouted.

Jack was incensed. 'Detention for us! What about her! She's an animal. She should be playing Wild Bill!'

But Mad lived in this crazy world where girls had to be protected and taken care of. No wonder they called him Mad!

'Are you all right, dear?' he kept asking Lizzie. She fluttered her spots at him.

47

'Yes, sir,' she said softly.

'We should have her charged with assault!' Jack whispered to Sandy.

Mad heard him. 'One more word out of you boys. One more giggle. Just one more and I promise you, you'll both be playing chorus girls.' Mad's eyes flashed. 'Am I making myself clear?'

Both boys nodded. However, it was really hard to keep from giggling when Angus Paige came on. The poor boy just couldn't stop sneezing.

'I've got an allergy,' he explained to Mad when the teacher warned him that the next time he sneezed he would put a bag over his head.

When Angus finally went into his song, the teacher insisted he wear a female wig. That made Jack and Sandy go into a fit of the giggles again.

'I think he'd look better with a bag over his head,' Jack said to Sandy.

To make things worse, every time Angus sneezed, the wig either fell off or slid over his face. He was a disaster.

Mad was almost in tears. 'Angus,' he said, when he'd finished, 'You're abysmal.'

Angus smiled. 'Thank you, sir.'

Jack turned to Sandy, puzzled. 'I thought he was rubbish.'

Lizzie Ferrier tapped him on the shoulder. 'Abysmal means rubbish. Stupid!'

'Clever clogs!' he said back. 'I never heard anybody saying they put their abysmal into the bin!'

Lizzie tutted. 'Stupid,' she said again.

Mad was calling for order from the stage. 'Jack Tarrant.' He was holding a note in his hand that someone had just handed him.

'Yessir.' Jack jumped to his feet, eager to please.

'A message from your mum.' He put on his glasses and read it out very slowly. 'You've to go home with Lizzie Ferrier tonight. Your mum will collect you later.'

Jack wished the ground would open up and swallow everyone in the hall except him. He was dead embarrassed.

A cheer went up, a few whistles, shouts, even a chant – 'Jack and Lizzie, Jack and Lizzie.' He wanted to die. What was his mother thinking about?

Someone shouted, 'I think you'd better take karate lessons if you're going home with her.'

'He doesn't need karate lessons. Lizzie'll take care of him.'

Lizzie couldn't resist it. 'Yes, I'll take care of him . . . till his mummy comes to collect him!'

And the chant rose. 'Mummy's boy! Mummy's boy!'

Even Mad was laughing. There was uproar in the hall. Everyone was laughing. Even Jack was laughing. Laughing to hide the humiliation. Could none of them see how it hurt him? Inside he was

49

screaming. Screaming at them all. At his pals, at his teacher, at Lizzie.

Most of all, at his mother!

12

*L*izzie's mother was ironing when Jack arrived. She only had a part-time job and was always home when Lizzie came back from school. Lizzie was already in, sprawled along the sofa in the living room reading some stupid book. He had been determined not to walk from school with her. No way!

'I've got one of those,' he said, throwing himself down on the chair.

Lizzie pretended amazement. 'A book! You! What do you use it for? Propping up your bed?'

'At least I don't have to read out loud.'

That was her soft spot. Her eyes flashed at him. She was almost off the couch and at him, but her mother coming in from the kitchen saved him.

'You two always have something to say to each other. You get on so well.'

The poor woman believed that too! 'I just said so to your mother, Jack. Of course Jack can come here, I said. Him and my Lizzie get on so well.'

Lizzie looked at Jack. If she hadn't been snarling at him, he was convinced she would have giggled too.

'Where *is* my mum?' He didn't want to ask in front of Lizzie, but he had to know.

'Oh, she's really busy. Doesn't know when she'll get home. Working late.'

Very vague, he thought. Not like Big Rose at all.

Mrs Ferrier was not half so much fun as his mother. No wonder Lizzie was such a bore. Mrs Ferrier took everything very seriously, even her ironing.

'Can't possibly make the tea till I redo these blouses.' She had taken one just to show them how much they'd creased since she'd ironed them ten minutes before. They looked fine to Jack. Lizzie, however, was appalled.

'That's awful, Mum. It's that material. It creases so easily.'

I've died and gone to hell, Jack decided. Nobody alive could have a conversation about the creases in a blouse!

Consequently, tea was very late. The news was on television as they ate.

'I mean, no wonder they escape from prison. That one was on a work detail outside. They thought he was harmless! Harmless? Would you look at that face. It's got evil written all over it. Isn't he frightening?'

Mrs Ferrier was referring to the armed robber, still on the run. The picture flashed on the screen of an unsmiling villain. Lizzie glanced from the screen to Jack.

'I've seen worse,' she said.

'It's a frightening world,' Mrs Ferrier went on. 'Things are getting worse all the time. I wish that boy of mine would hurry up and come home.'

'That boy' was her son, Eddie – Lizzie's brother. Sixteen and at the local college.

'We've got police patrols on our street,' Jack said. 'Have you?'

Mrs Ferrier looked a little put out. 'Have you? I'm going to phone the council and demand we get them too.' So, they obviously didn't have a police patrol then. 'It's because of this assault. An elderly woman, can you believe it? And in her own house! And the police still don't have a clue who did it. Can you believe it?'

His mother was late. It was almost nine before she came for him, full of apologies to Mrs Ferrier and to Jack. He thought she looked flustered and a little pale.

'Don't worry about it, Rose,' Mrs Ferrier assured her. 'He's a pleasure to have, isn't he, Lizzie?'

Lizzie had to force her head to nod in agreement.

Jack stood up straight, flicked at his collar. 'I can't help it,' he said. 'I always have that affect on women.'

Mrs Ferrier giggled. 'See what I mean? He just has you laughing all the time.'

'Oh, he's a barrel of laughs,' Big Rose said.

And as the two women continued to talk, Lizzie turned to him and prodded his belly. 'Well, you're a barrel anyway.'

Jack hardly spoke to his mother on the way home, till finally she asked, 'Is there something wrong with you?'

'Something wrong? Do you know that note of yours was read out in front of the whole school? Lizzie Ferrier will never let me forget that. You know I can't stand her!'

'I'm sorry. I didn't mean them to do that. I'm really sorry, Jack.'

'Where were you anyway?' And before she could answer, he answered for her. 'Out with Alec?'

She seemed to hesitate, or was she concentrating on the traffic as they crossed the street? 'Yes,' she said at last.

'So why are we walking home? He might have collected me in his car and dropped us both off.'

She hadn't thought of that, which wasn't like

Big Rose at all. 'He was in a hurry, and if I don't mind the walk, neither should you.'

She was lying. But why? What was going on?

The house lay in darkness as they went in, but there was a heat in the living room, as if the fire had been on recently.

'So where did you and Alec go?' he asked casually.

'We went for a nice meal and a drive,' she answered just as casually.

'You might have brought him home for a coffee.'

'Well, I didn't. OK? What is this, the third degree?'

He shrugged and went into the kitchen to pour himself a glass of milk.

And there on the draining board stood two upturned mugs.

Big mistake, Mother.

Fire in the living room. Two mugs drying in the kitchen.

Someone had been here. And it must have been Alec. His mother didn't know any other men.

The question was, why was she lying about it?

13

*A*t breakfast next morning his mother was very quiet.

'Are you all right, Mum?'

She pushed her cornflakes around her bowl and looked up at him. 'I think I might have a cold coming on,' she said.

Big Rose never caught cold, never had anything wrong with her. 'Why can't I be ill for a change?' she'd sometimes moan. 'Then I could get time off work like everybody else.'

Now, she had a cold coming on.

'Maybe you should stay off work,' he suggested. When she didn't answer, he added hopefully, 'I could stay off school too. I think I might have a cold coming on as well.'

'Yes, and pigs might fly.'

Jack shrugged. 'No way? Is that what you're trying to say?'

She snatched his half-eaten flakes away from him. 'Words to that effect, dear. Now, you get upstairs and brush your teeth.'

*

He was on his way out the door when he remembered Sandy had asked him for his badminton racket. He hauled on the cellar door. It didn't budge.

'Mum!' he called. 'I can't get into the cellar. It's locked.'

She appeared at the kitchen door, pulling on her coat.

'I've locked it,' she said. 'That top stair broke completely yesterday. I almost broke my neck. So nobody's going down there till I get a joiner to fix it.'

'Oh go on, Mum. Sandy wants a loan of my racket. I'll be careful, honest.'

She grabbed him by the shoulders and hauled him to the front door. 'Sandy can get his own badminton racket. Now you, off to school.'

He had little time to think about his mother, because there was so much going on in school that day.

The police came. Two of them, coming in to each class asking if any of them had been in the vicinity of the assault on the elderly woman. Two children had been seen. They might have seen something. Jack racked his brain. He wanted desperately to be one of those children. He tried to convince himself he had been in the area, though he couldn't even remember what night it had been. Imagine! If he could only solve the crime for the police. His picture would be all over the front pages. He would be a hero.

It appeared as if Joe Grady was reading his thoughts. 'Couldn't have been you,' he sneered. 'I mean, you've got a perfect alibi. You were out with your mummy, as usual.'

Jack snarled back at him. 'Maybe it's you and Lizzie they're looking for.' He began to chant softly. 'I'm in a tizzy over Lizzie. I'm in a tizzy over Lizzie.' Sandy and some of his classmates began to giggle.

Joe was furious, baring his teeth like an angry ape. 'I'm going to get you for that later, Tarrant.'

Jack only laughed and added to his chant. 'Even though her zits are the pits.'

That made Joe decide not to wait till later. He was suddenly flying at Jack. Jack yelped and fell back, and chaos broke out in the classroom.

Above the noise, all Jack could hear was Miss Potts's squeaky voice. 'See these boys, officers, they're always fighting over this girl.'

Jack tried to get his mouth free to yell that he was *not* fighting over Lizzie Ferrier. No way! In fact, he wasn't fighting at all. He was getting mutilated by Joe Grady.

Suddenly, the two policemen hauled them both to their feet.

'It was his fault, sir,' Joe screamed, still struggling.

'He jumped me.' Jack defended himself, trying to sound innocent. 'I didn't do anything, sir.'

Miss Potts squealed again. 'I've never been so mortified in all my life.' She stamped her tiny feet. 'Joe Grady! Jack Tarrant! You are both going to be reported to the headmaster for this!'

One of the policemen turned at the mention of Jack's name. 'Are you Jack Tarrant?' His eyes were curious. He looked at him for a moment. It seemed a long time to Jack. Then he let him go and made his way out of the class again.

Jack hadn't answered him. Couldn't have if he'd tried. He had heard that voice before. It was the voice of the inspector he'd heard talking to his mother on the phone.

14

*H*e got a green slip. That was pretty bad. You got one of those when you had behaved with severe impro- impro- well, when you behaved very badly anyway.

As he walked home, he was trying to decide exactly how he would tell Big Rose about the green slip. Best form of defence, he decided, was definitely attack.

'Me and Joe had to be separated by a big policeman.' He imagined himself telling her. 'You know the one, he was on the phone to you the other night.' Then he could watch for her reaction. That might be the very thing to do. She'd have to explain why she'd been behaving so strangely lately.

She was in when he arrived home. The house was filled with the smell of spaghetti bolognese – his favourite.

'Mama mia. I'm home!' he shouted, getting into the mood for the Italian nosh.

She suddenly appeared from the kitchen with a red-checked tea towel wrapped round her head like an Italian peasant. 'Asta la vista manyana!' she answered. He knew that was gibberish. She couldn't speak Italian. She made him laugh anyway.

'Meala ready tena minutes,' she continued, and disappeared into the kitchen again.

He ran up the stairs. He'd tell her after tea about the green slip. He wasn't going to let anything spoil his spaghetti bolognese. He opened his bedroom door – and the first thing he saw was his badminton racket. The one that he kept in the cellar. The cellar that just that morning had been too dangerous for anyone to go down.

*

'I thought that was your favourite?' his mum asked him, watching him push his spaghetti round the plate with his fork.

He looked up at her, wanting to see her reaction as he spoke. 'You get that step fixed in the cellar then?'

'No,' she said at once, puzzled. 'And you keep away from the cellar. I don't want you to fall and break your neck.'

'You must have taken a chance going down there.'

She looked totally baffled. 'I'm not going down there either, pal. I can't afford to break a leg. I'm a one-parent family. I have to work.' She laughed, expecting him to laugh with her. He didn't. 'That's why I've got it locked.'

'You've not been down there then?'

'I told you. It's locked and that's that.'

He sat in silence for a moment.

'Well, what is it now?' she asked at last.

He was wondering whether to ask her. Curiosity won in the end. 'So how did my badminton racket get into my bedroom? Magic?'

He took her completely by surprise. He had never seen Big Rose so gobsmacked before. Only for a few seconds though. Suddenly, she was Big Rose again, sure of herself, in control, funny. She was good, his mother.

'Who do you think I am, Paul Daniels? I got

your badminton racket out, risking life and limb, I might tell you. What a mother! I hope you appreciate me.'

'I thought you said –'

'I knew you needed it.' She cut him off, not wanting to talk about it. 'Now eat up your spaghetti. If it lies there any longer it'll breed maggots.'

They didn't speak of it again, in fact they hardly spoke at all. He didn't tell her about the green slip. He forgot all about it. All he kept thinking about was that his mum had lied . . . again.

She knew nothing about the badminton racket in his bedroom. That had taken her completely by surprise. She certainly hadn't taken it from the cellar.

And the thing that puzzled him, worried him and most of all terrified him, was: if she didn't do it, who did?

15

'Maybe you've got a ghost!' Sandy said after Jack had told him all that had happened. He had to tell someone. He couldn't keep it to himself. They were in the school playground during morning break.

'A ghost?' Jack replied. 'Must have been a really thoughtful ghost bringing my badminton racket up from the cellar so I wouldn't fall and hurt myself.'

'Have you got a dicey step in the cellar?'

Jack thought about that. 'I never knew we had, but my mum said —'

'I wouldn't take her word for it,' Sandy told him.

Jack was almost ready for a fight at that. It was all right for him to think his mother had lied, but anyone else . . . no way!

Sandy leaned closer and whispered. 'Women do a lot of funny things, especially mothers. Mine talks to herself constantly. She looks like a halfwit. Always blames it on her age.'

'But Big Rose is different.'

And she was. She didn't do any of the daft, unexplainable things other mothers did. She was straight down the middle, his mother. Always told him the truth. At least, until now.

'Well, what do you think then? Maybe she's got a mad relative down there.'

'She's more likely to have a man down there. She's always threatening to kidnap Mel Gibson.'

'Maybe that's who it is then. Nothing in the paper about him going missing?' Sandy giggled. So did Jack. But the thought remained. There was only one way to solve the mystery. He was going down the cellar himself. He had to find out what it was she didn't want him to discover down there.

At lunchtime, he went home. He never did that. He always had dinner at school. But he knew his mother didn't come home either. Wouldn't expect him to. A perfect time for a little exploring.

The house seemed especially quiet in the mid-day sun. The pendulum clock in the hallway ticked the time away. Jack stepped into the hall and listened. The silence seemed almost eerie.

Rubbish!

He wiped that thought away immediately. There was nothing eerie about this house. This was his house. He'd lived here almost all his life, almost as far back as he could remember. He loved it.

Yet, here, in the daylight, in the sunshine, for the very first time, it was creepy, and he couldn't brush the feeling away.

He straightened his shoulders and marched into the kitchen to get a torch.

The key to the cellar door normally hung on a rack in the kitchen. Now it was missing. He stood for a moment trying to figure out how he would get in. The door was probably too strong to knock in with his shoulder. Anyway, he'd only ever seen that done in films and Big Rose said in real life you'd be more likely to break your shoulder than the door.

He had to get into that cellar. He knew now he wouldn't leave the house and go back to school without finding out why his mum had locked the cellar door. He hoped it was just because of a broken step. It had to be. There had been a duplicate key to the cellar. Whatever had happened to it? He searched through a kitchen drawer where Mum kept screwdrivers and an assortment of old rusty keys.

'Why don't you ever throw these out?' he had once asked her.

'Because you never know when they might come in handy,' had been her answer.

Like today, Jack thought. He palmed three likely candidates. Long and thin, they looked exactly alike, and identical to the cellar key.

The first one wouldn't even turn in the lock. For a moment he was sure the second one was going to work. He turned it several times and it seemed just about to catch, but never did.

Only one left. One last chance, and if that didn't work . . . then what would he do? Could he pick the lock, he wondered?

He was so busy considering his lock-picking skills that he didn't realize the last key had caught. The lock turned, the door opened.

The steps leading down to the cellar yawned into blackness.

This was it, he thought. Now or never.

Jack took one tentative step . . . and began to go down.

16

Why did the cellar light have to be at the bottom of the stairs? Jack wanted to flood the place with light now; see into every nook and every cranny. He switched on the torch but its solitary, pathetic beam only reached as far as the bottom of the stairs.

There was no broken step here. The first lie. What else had she lied about? He took another step.

Was that a sound? A movement?

He shone the torch around, but the beam was too weak. He could see nothing. It had probably been a mouse. They'd never had mice before. But there was a first time for everything. Isn't that what they said?

Another step.

And another.

Then he stopped to listen.

Silence. Too much silence?

Like an old television western.

It's too quiet, pardner.

What a load of rubbish! Of course it was quiet! There was nobody here.

He almost tripped on the last step and the beam of his torch wavered and wobbled till he steadied himself. He reached out for the light switch. Found it. Flicked it down.

Nothing happened.

He flicked it up and down a few times before he decided it wasn't working. Was that why Mum had locked the cellar? Then why not say so. Why the nonsense, the lie, about the broken step?

No. There was something else here. He flashed the torch around the cellar. The usual boxes, his old bike. Goodness, had he ever been that small? His mother's exercise bike, hardly used.

Memories. That's what they kept down in the cellar. There was his snooker table. The first time he'd used it he'd ripped the felt.

He laughed as he remembered his mother's reaction to that.

'Bang goes my dream of being the mother of the next Stephen Hendry!'

He was still laughing as he turned the beam on to the bed in the corner.

THE BED IN THE CORNER!

That shouldn't be there. His Spiderman duvet

lay crumpled on it. As if someone had been lying there, just a moment ago.

Jack held his breath.

A movement to the right of him. This time he wasn't mistaken. He gasped and swung the torch round the floor.

A mouse! A rat even. Let it be one of them. A whole pack of them.

A pair of shoes.

He began to move the light upwards. Trousers, blue.

Jack was shaking. He couldn't stop.

Up and up. To someone breathing almost as quickly as Jack.

Every instinct told him to run. Throw the torch, run. Why couldn't he move? Why was he glued to the cellar floor?

And finally . . . the light fell on a face, blinking against the beam of the torch.

Jack let out a low yelp and took a step back.

He'd seen that face before. Recognized it. And it frightened him.

The figure took a menacing step toward Jack, and in that instant everything fell into place.

He remembered where he had seen that face.

It was the face he'd seen on television every night for the past week. The face of the armed robber who was on the run from the police.

17

*T*he escaped criminal had been hiding in their cellar! He'd probably threatened Mum unless she let him stay there.

Jack let out a yell and turned and ran. He heard a quick movement behind him, felt the hand reach out and grab for him. Jack was too quick, almost throwing himself at the stairs, taking them two at a time.

His breath was coming in short gasps. He wanted to shout out, to scream at the top of his voice, but he needed all his breath to get away. To get up those stairs and out of this cellar.

At the top step he tripped and felt hands grip at his trousers. He tried to yank himself free but the grip grew tighter, the hand encircling his ankle. Jack turned and saw the face. It was even more frightening this close. Icy-blue eyes, teeth gritted together with determination. Determination that Jack would never leave this cellar.

The man opened his mouth to speak. Said one word. 'Wait . . .' When, suddenly, Jack remembered the torch, still clutched in his hand. He hurled it hard against the man's head. It caught him right between those icy eyes and he let out a yell and let Jack go. Jack was up and off, wasting no time, racing for the top of the stairs. He would have locked the door, but the man was already staggering to his feet. Too close.

No. Jack decided to run for the front door, the street, safety.

He was almost there. His hand was already on the handle when suddenly he was grabbed from behind. Jack struggled as he'd never struggled before, kicking against the man, hearing him mutter, 'No. Wait. Listen.'

Jack was doing none of those things. When the man's hand was thrust around his mouth, Jack bit hard into the flesh. So hard he could taste blood. The man yelled, let go again and Jack grabbed once more for the door.

He yanked it open – and there stood his mother, key in hand, ready to come in.

Jack ran at her and almost knocked her off her feet. 'Run, Mum! It's him! On the telly! Quick!' He tried to push her out.

She looked stunned, puzzled, as if she couldn't take it all in.

'Mum! Run!'

He grabbed at her to pull her outside with him, and suddenly, she had his arm and was pulling him back inside!

Closing the door softly behind her. Locking

them both back inside with . . . *no*! He still struggled against her, not understanding. Afraid.

'Mum! What are you doing?'

The man stood, sucking on his hand. But he didn't look the least bit worried that his mother was there now.

Jack looked back at his mother. She looked as if she was ready to cry. And that really would have panicked him more than anything else. His mother didn't do things like that.

'Mum?' he said again.

His mother was looking at the man with real venom in her eyes. 'I hate you for this,' she said at last.

The man looked back at her. 'You should have told him, Rosie.'

Jack almost collapsed. This villain, this criminal, this . . . he had called his mother Rosie?

'Mum! Do you know him?'

His mother bit her lip and looked from the man to Jack. Looked at him for a long time.

'Oh, Jack,' she murmured. She took a deep breath before she said the words that would change his life. 'He's your father, Jack.'

18

Jack felt his knees go weak. He really did. His mouth hung open. He looked at his mother. 'I haven't got a father,' he managed to say at last.

She shook her head. 'He's your father,' she repeated.

He wouldn't believe it. He couldn't. 'My dad's dead. You told me.'

'She lied.' The man stepped closer and Jack moved back beside his mother.

This man. His father? No way!

'Do you blame me?' Mum shouted. 'What was I supposed to say. "By the way, son, the reason you don't actually see your father is because he's in jail for armed robbery and serious assault." '

'You could have told him I was innocent!' The man shouted back.

'I'd have to believe that first.' She threw the words at him.

'Of course, Rosie. Believing in me was always too much for you.'

Rosie! He had called her it again.

'I fell for that "I'm innocent" rubbish too often to fall for it again.'

They were arguing with each other as if he wasn't there. Jack was suddenly as angry as they were. 'Will you two shut up! What's happening? What's he doing here?'

His mother squeezed his shoulder drawing him to her. 'I'm sorry, Jack. I couldn't tell you. You were only a baby when he went away. I didn't want you growing up with everyone knowing what your father was. So I moved away, changed my name, made a new life for us here. A good life!' She said that defiantly, daring the man to deny it.

'I made one mistake,' she went on. 'I let your grandfather know where I was.'

Jack couldn't believe his ears! 'Wait a minute, I've got a grandfather as well?' One minute he was the child of a one-parent family. The next he had a whole tribe to contend with.

'My dad,' the man said softly. There was almost a smile in his voice. 'You'd like him. She does.' He nodded to his mother.

'He's going to hear it from me for telling you where I lived. He promised he'd never do that.'

'Do you know how hard it's been for him? You told him where you were, and then you made him promise never to contact you, or see you, or Jack. And he's done that. All these years, he's kept out of your life. Because he knows how hard it's been for you, Rosie.'

'So why did he have to tell you now?' she demanded, angrily.

'Because this is my last chance to see Jack. And he knows it. I made him tell me, Rosie. I had to know.'

'Why?' She was yelling now. 'So you could do this to us? Involve us in your escape? Do you know the trouble you could cause for us?'

'I'm sorry.' He said it to Jack. 'I'm sorry, son.'

'Don't call me "son",' Jack shouted. 'I'm not your son.'

'I had nowhere else to go. I only planned to stay a day or two. See you, but Big Rose here –'

He'd called her Big Rose now. Jack was the only person in the world who had ever called his mother Big Rose.

'She'd gone to the police, hadn't she? Told them who she was. Asked them to keep an eye on the house in case I did find out where you were.'

The visits to the police station, the police patrols. It all fell into place now.

'It didn't do you any harm.' Mum was almost laughing. 'The police weren't to know you'd already found us. This will be the last place they'll look for you now.'

'And it's because they're watching all the time

I can't get away. So don't blame it all on me.'

'And who am I going to blame? It's all your fault. Everything's your fault.'

He hung his head. Said nothing. He probably couldn't argue with that. 'I'll go as soon as I can,' he said at last. 'I promise.' He looked at Jack. 'But I had to see him. I wanted to see my son.'

'You've seen him. Now go.'

'Why don't you just tell the police he's here?' Jack said. 'Get them to come and take him?'

That was what Jack couldn't understand. Mum going off to work each day, and not taking the chance to turn him in.

'I can't go back there, Jack,' the man said. 'I've been in jail for eleven years for something I didn't do.'

'Funny how no one's ever believed that,' his mother snapped.

'Some people did. My dad did, eventually. And there's a reporter trying to get enough evidence to get the case opened up again. But when I was turned down for parole, Jack –' He was pleading with him, wanting him to believe him too – 'that was it. I had to get out. I'm never going back there.'

Jack looked at his mother. She was staring straight ahead. 'You don't believe him, do you?'

She said nothing, but her shrug said it all.

'Well why don't we just go to the police? Tell them he's here. They can come and get him anytime.'

That was the kind of thing he would have expected his mother, Big Rose, to do. Instead, a little tear began to trickle down her cheek.

'I can't, Jack,' she said softly. 'I just can't.'

'Well, I'll tell!' Jack shouted. 'You see if I don't. I hate you! I hate both of you!'

And he bounded up the stairs to his room and slammed the door.

What was he going to do?

What could he possibly do?

19

*T*en minutes later there was a knock on his door.

'Can I come in?'

His mother didn't wait for an answer, opening the door and peering round. She looked as if she'd been crying. That disturbed Jack more than anything else. 'Can I?' she asked again.

' 'Spose,' he muttered, turning away from her on the bed. He could still see her in the mirror, wringing her hands and biting her lip. This wasn't his mother! His mother didn't do things like this! What was happening?

'I'm sorry, Jack. You've every reason to be angry with me. I thought I was doing the right thing.'

He didn't say anything for a while; didn't know what to say.

'I thought I didn't have a dad,' he managed to mutter at last.

'Would it have been better to know you did have one? That he was a jailbird?'

He didn't know the answer to that either.

'Is he really a bad man?'

He'd heard it night after night on the news, and yet he'd hardly listened. Remembered just snatches of 'Do not approach. Could be dangerous. Responsible for vicious assault during armed robbery.' Yet, other snatches were confusing. 'Exemplary behaviour while in custody.'

What kind of a man was he?

Big Rose didn't seem to know either.

'He was wild when I first knew him, Jack,' she began, sitting on the bed beside him. 'I was seventeen. He was eighteen. He was up to everything. Hot-wiring cars, joyriding, driving too fast. Nothing really bad. He never hurt anyone. He was never in fights or anything. Then we got married and you were born. And for a while everything was brilliant. That was the best time. That man could charm the birds off the trees.'

She was quiet for a minute, remembering. There was even the hint of a smile on her face. Then, just as suddenly, it was gone. She closed her eyes tight, as if she was trying to blot out something awful.

'Then he lost his job. Money was really tight. He couldn't get another one, we couldn't pay the mortgage. And that was when he started hanging out with a really bad crowd. I kept on and on at him to keep away from them. He said I was nagging. And I was.'

She sat up straight. 'And quite blinking right I was too! They were planning a robbery and got your stupid father to join in on it. And look what happened. I told him then I'd never forgive him, and I won't! I won't!'

She rubbed at her eyes like a little girl determined not to cry.

'He said he was innocent. He didn't do it,' said Jack.

'He always maintained that. Said he backed out at the last minute. Unfortunately, the other three who were at the robbery said he was the fourth man. He always said they were protecting someone else. Maybe if he'd had an alibi . . .' She sighed, shrugged her shoulders. 'But he didn't. He

wasn't at home with his wife and son at the time.
Maybe if he had been . . .'

She sounded really bitter about that.

Jack turned on the bed to face her. 'So if you
hate him that much, why didn't you turn him
in when you found him here? You could have
pretended to go to work and gone to the police
instead. You could have shopped him.'

'I know. I could have. I should have.' Another
big sigh. 'But you know, Jack. The first time I saw
him when I was seventeen, I was absolutely
bowled over by him. Those big blue eyes, just like
yours. And your sense of humour too. I was crazy
about him from the first time I laid my eyes on
him.'

He tried to imagine his mother bowled over by
a boy, even one as good looking as Jack himself.
He couldn't picture it.

'And do you still feel like that about him?'

That remark shocked her. 'No, I do not! I hate
him, but because of the way I used to feel I just
couldn't go to the police.' She looked at Jack for
understanding. 'He's going Jack. Give him a
couple of days and he'll be out of our lives for
ever.'

'And is that what you want?' he asked her.

'Oh yes, Jack.' She sounded as if she meant it.
'I want him out of our lives. Then we can get
everything back to normal.'

78

Jack, however, had the feeling that for him nothing would ever be normal again.

20

*J*ack didn't come downstairs again that night. Mum brought his tea up to his room. And next morning, at breakfast, it was just him and Big Rose.

'Has he gone?' he asked finally. He had even begun to imagine, wish, he had dreamed the whole thing. It had never really happened.

His mother shattered that dream. 'He's in the cellar.'

'Good!' he said at once. 'I hope he stays there. I don't want to see him.'

He gobbled down his breakfast. He wanted to get away from the house, away from his mother's guilty look.

'You'll be OK at school?' she asked as he was leaving. Mum had phoned to say he'd been unwell the day before, to explain his afternoon absence.

'Just act normally,' she added, then she was laughing. 'You, act normally? That would be a dead giveaway. Just act your usual mad self. They all think you're daft as a brush at that school anyway.'

He was smiling now too. Couldn't help it. 'How do you do that, Mum?'

'Do what?' she asked.

'You make jokes. You make me laugh. You've been hiding him in the cellar for days, and you've still been joking. How do you do that?'

A voice answered them from inside the hallway. His voice. 'She always could make me laugh too. Even when things were really bad. She's good, Big Rose, isn't she?'

Jack turned and looked at him. THIS MAN IS DANGEROUS. The thought leapt at him from a newspaper headline, yet here he was standing in his hall with his hands round a hot mug of coffee, calling his mother Big Rose, and talking about her as if he knew her as well as Jack did.

'You see, Jack,' he went on, 'when you make people laugh, they don't see how you're feeling deep down inside.'

That was true. Jack had always covered all the hurt about being called a 'mummy's boy' by being the class clown. The funny one. He was just like Mum.

But how did the stranger know that?

He didn't think, however, he could be the funny one today.

'You look very pale, Jack. Are you still not well?' His French teacher asked solicitously. '*Peutêtre*, you should have stayed off *aujourd'hui* as well, dear.'

'Poor *petit* Jack,' Lizzie Ferrier taunted as they left French. 'No jokes today? Not so jolly, eh? Well, never *jolie*, actually. Jolly ugly in fact.'

All her mates giggled at her wit.

'Wait till you hear what Jack's going to say to you, HA!' Sandy shouted, then turned to his pal. 'Come on, Jack. Say something nasty about her zits.'

Jack shrugged and moved off down the corridor while Lizzie leapt in the air, victorious for once.

'You really are sick,' Sandy said, peering at him for signs of feverishness or spots. 'What's wrong?'

'Just don't feel right,' Jack answered, glad at least of an excuse for it all.

Yet every time anyone looked at him he was sure they must be able to read the guilt in his face.

'*I am hiding an escaped convict in my cellar.*'

He was sure it was written in lights on his forehead.

There were rehearsals for the show after school. Jack didn't want to go. He almost made an excuse for going home, until he remembered exactly what awaited him at home, and he changed his mind.

There wasn't much for him and Sandy to do

anyway, except wave their guns in the air and shout 'BANG!' (They were not allowed caps until the night of the show itself.) He couldn't work up any enthusiasm for that either. Angus was still rubbish, and when Lizzie began to sing 'Secret Love' off-key, all that managed to do was bring a smile to his lips.

Joe Grady noticed even that. 'You laughing at Lizzie's singing?' he snarled.

'Oh, so that's what it was. I thought she was miming to a cat being strangled.'

Sandy was delighted. His pal was feeling better.

'What did you say?' Joe did his best to look menacing.

Jack could see it all. He would throw another insult. Joe would throw a punch. Then Lizzie would come along and join in. Suddenly, he couldn't be bothered.

'Nothing. Sorry. I didn't mean it.' And to Sandy's extreme disappointment, he moved to another part of the hall.

'He's sick,' Sandy explained to everyone. 'Jack's not been well.' And he muttered as he followed after him. 'He must be . . . to miss a chance to insult Lizzie Ferrier.'

21

*H*e was sitting at the kitchen table when Jack went home, eating his tea, as if he belonged there.

'I'm sorry,' he said, standing up. 'Would you prefer me to go back down to the cellar?'

Before Jack could answer, his mother said, 'Don't be silly. Finish your tea.' She looked at Jack. 'The blinds are drawn. No one can see him. It's perfectly safe.'

Jack glared at her. 'I can see him.'

He threw down his rucksack. He wanted them to know how angry he was; making him a party to this. He still hated them both. He yanked open the door of the refrigerator and pulled out the milk.

'You didn't say anything?' his mother asked softly.

That annoyed him more than anything. 'If I had the place would be surrounded by cops.' He snapped the words out. 'Anyway, I'm not a grass.'

'Of course he isn't.' The man smiled at him.

Jack refused to think of him as his father. He wasn't his father.

'I didn't do it for you.' He had never been so cheeky before. But he had cause, didn't he?

The man sighed and looked away.

'OK, you've made your point,' his mother said. 'Now, take your milk and go into the living room. I'll bring your tea in there.'

She didn't want him to stay. He thought he could understand why. She didn't want him to get to know the man at all. Well, that suited Jack.

'Rose was saying you're in the school show. *Calamity Jane*?'

Jack didn't answer. He just looked at him, waiting for him to go into his version of 'The Deadwood Stage'.

It was as if the man read his thoughts. 'Don't worry. I'm not going to sing "The Deadwood Stage". What is it about that song?' He was smiling again, hoping maybe that Jack might smile back. Jack didn't.

'Bet you wish I'd get on it – and leave town.'

Now that almost did bring a smile to Jack's lips. He was sure the man could see it.

'You're in the school football team as well?'

Jack shrugged. 'So?'

'He's about as good as you used to be,' his mother said.

The man looked at her. 'That bad, eh?' Then his glance went back to Jack. 'Does she boost you up like that as well? She always knew how to put the boot in, did Rosie. Anyway, I wasn't that bad.'

'Huh! you're not supposed to handle the ball in football,' she threw at him.

'I always got it mixed up with rugby.' He looked at Jack and lifted an eyebrow.

'Even in rugby you don't run off the pitch with it and try to sell it to another team.'

'I only did that once.' He was smiling broadly now.

'Once was enough to ruin his footballing career, Jack.' His mother directed her words at Jack. 'Of course, forging the Celtic team's autographs on it didn't go down too well either.'

'They raffled it for charity.' This time he chanced a smile at Big Rose. 'Made them a bomb.'

Did Big Rose smile back? For a second Jack thought she had. Was this her being bowled over? She certainly hid it well. In an instant the grimness was back in her face.

'Jack!' she ordered. 'Get into the living room!'

'When Big Rose gives an order you've got to obey pronto, eh, Jack?' The man leaned back in his chair as if he was thoroughly enjoying it all. 'I think she did her training with the SS, eh? Jah, *Mein Führer*!'

Rose glared at him. 'And you shut up and finish your tea!'

*

Jack lay in bed that night thinking. Was that the way it might have been if his father – his father? He still couldn't get used to using that word – if he hadn't been a jailbird? Him and his mother and . . .

Jack could see how he could fit in with them. He was funny too. He knew how to handle his mother, just the way Jack did. Maybe, if things had been different . . .

He pushed the pictures that were crowding into his mind out for ever. Pictures of family and fun and fathers.

He didn't have a father.

He had a dangerous convict who meant nothing to him, hiding out in his cellar. Soon he would go out of their lives for ever, and good riddance! He'd had no right to come here. He had put them into a dangerous position. That was how much he cared about his son, his wife.

Jack was suddenly frightened of what might happen if the police found out he was here, and that they had been hiding him.

Would they send his mother to jail?

Would he be put in a home?

He had always wanted an adventure in his life, longed for one. But not this. This was too scary. This was too real.

He hated that man in the cellar. Hated him.

22

*T*hey were in the maths class next day when the police car drew up outside the window.

Sandy saw it first. 'Hey! Wonder what the cops are doing here?'

Jack felt the colour drain from his face and his knees go weak.

Lizzie noticed. 'Don't look so worried,' she said. 'They can't arrest you for being ugly.'

'Maybe it's you they're after,' Jack snapped back at her. 'They've heard about your singing. Noise pollution. Danger to the environment.'

She made a face at him and turned her attention back to the window and the four policemen getting out of their car.

The whole class had moved to the window to watch. Poor old Dunn, the maths teacher was banging frantically on his desk trying to bring their attention back to geometry. Finally, he gave up and joined them at the window.

Only Jack still sat in his seat, feeling sick. Why had they come? Come here to the school? Only one answer sprang to his mind.

They knew.

Maybe he had let it slip to a teacher without realizing. Maybe they had seen it in his face, seen the guilt, been suspicious of his strange behaviour.

'What's wrong with you, Jack?' Mr Dunn noticed him at last. He knew Jack would normally be among the first to jump to the window for a front-row view. 'Are you feeling all right?'

'No, sir!' He leapt at once on the excuse. 'I feel really sick, sir. Can I go to the toilet?'

Jack made a face, covered his mouth with his hand as if he was about to spew all over the desk.

Mr Dunn looked disgusted. He snatched Jack's maths jotter out of range. 'Yes. I think perhaps you'd better.'

Jack kept his hand over his mouth and ran from the classroom as fast as he could, before he became the focus of the class's attention and not the police.

He ran down the corridor with no intention at all of heading for the toilets. He was making for the nearest exit. He was going home. And once there, he was going to pack a bag and leave.

Why had HE ever had to come here and do this to them?

Were the police even now at Mum's work, handcuffing her, taking her in? Had she been arrested, the house raided? He had to get home to find out!

He put on a spurt as he rounded a corner and

ran straight into the arms of one of the policemen.

He held Jack by the shoulders. 'Here, young man, where are you going in such a hurry?'

Jack tried to answer, but his mouth was too dry. Jack could only stare at him, feel the beads of sweat forming on his brow. They *must* see it in his face. He imagined the handcuffs being clapped on him at any minute.

The policeman smiled. 'Can you tell us where the headmaster's office is?'

He didn't have to answer. The headmaster himself suddenly appeared, hurrying down the corridor.

'This way, officers. Would you like to speak to each class separately? Or shall I assemble them all in the hall?'

He noticed Jack then, still held in the clutches of one of the policemen. 'Jack Tarrant! What are you doing out of class?'

Jack found his voice at last, though it didn't sound particularly like his at all. 'I was feeling sick, sir. Mr Dunn told me to go to the toilet.'

'Well, you're heading in the wrong direction then, aren't you?' He pointed in the opposite direction. 'The toilets are thataway! And don't dare be sick anywhere else!'

Jack pulled himself free. The policeman winked and whispered. 'Schoolteachers haven't changed much since my day, eh, son?'

Then he was off, marching down the corridor with his colleagues, while the tiny headmaster had to run to keep up with them.

They hadn't come for him at all. The whole school was assembled in the hall and they were asked if anyone had any information about the assault on the pensioner who still lay unconscious in a local hospital.

Jack felt a lot better as he listened. They didn't know!

The crime had taken place in this area, the policemen told them, and children had been seen in the vicinity. The police were sure one of the pupils might have seen something without realizing the significance. They also said the crime was due to be shown on *Crime Scene* in the next few days. A reconstruction. The police wanted them all to watch it in case it helped someone remember something.

'A reconstruction! Brilliant! I wonder when they're filming it. We could get discovered.' Sandy was excited as they walked home, talking about it.

'You've got a sick mind, Sandy. This is serious stuff.'

'I know, but wouldn't it be great if we *had* seen something; if we could supply the clue that would catch the villain?'

Jack agreed. 'But I can't even remember what night it happened, can you?

Sandy thought about that. 'You know, Jack, it was just about the same time as you started hearing noises in your house.' Sandy's eyes widened. 'Hey, maybe you've got the criminal hiding in your cellar!'

Jack caught his breath. Gasped. Felt everything swim in front of his eyes. Sandy didn't notice; didn't think for a minute that could possibly be true. His imagination was making giant leaps where he was solving the crime for the police.

Yet, Sandy was right. HE had arrived in their house just about the same time as the assault had taken place. Was that a coincidence?

Or – and he could hardly bear to think of this – was Sandy right?

Was the man the police were looking for, the same man who was hiding in his cellar.

His father?

23

*H*e wanted desperately to ask his mother when he went home. But somehow, he just couldn't find the words. She was curled up in the armchair, hugging a cushion when he went in.

'Where is HE?' Jack asked.

She glanced down towards the cellar. 'I can't risk him being up here when the blinds are up. Daylight. He can come up later.'

'Don't want him to!' Jack snapped the words out.

His mother nodded. 'I know.' She watched him as he threw himself down on the chair across from her. 'Are you OK? You look so worried.'

'Oh, sorry. I've got a dangerous criminal down in my cellar. What right have I got to look worried?'

Any other mother would probably have apologized then, or even cried. Not Big Rose. She started to laugh. 'Oh well, as long as it's not bothering you.'

He smiled too. Yet even then, he couldn't say the thing he really wanted to say. They ate their dinner in the kitchen, neither of them talking the way they normally did.

'The police were at school today,' he said at last.

She sat up straight, stared at him. 'What for?'

'That assault. The old lady's still in a coma.'

'I know,' she said. 'It's awful.'

'I really got a fright, Mum. I thought for a minute they were coming for me. That they'd found out.'

She looked at him for a long moment, saying nothing. For a second he almost thought she might cry. But she didn't. 'I've got us in an awful mess, son,' she said at last. 'But I'll make it up to you. I promise. As soon as he goes.'

And he knew then he had to ask her. He couldn't keep it in a moment longer. HE had arrived. The old woman had been assaulted. Too much of a coincidence. Too much.

'Mum, he came here at the same time. He's bad. The television said he was bad. Do you think it could have been him that ... did that? Do you?'

Even before he'd finished his mother's eyes had grown wide with horror. Was she just realizing that? Or had she been suspicious too?

'Jack!' was all she said. All she had a chance to say. For there HE was, all of a sudden, standing in the doorway of the kitchen.

'I told you to stay in the cellar,' his mum said.

'The blinds are closed now. No one can see me. I want to speak to you, to both of you.'

Jack shouted, 'Don't want to hear anything you've got to say.'

'I can understand that. You don't even know who I am, Jack. I've never been there when you needed a father ... and I'm here now, and you don't want me.'

'He's never needed a father!' his mother said.

Jack knew that was wrong. He would have loved a father. But not one like this.

'But you've got to know. I've never hurt anyone. I'd never hurt anyone. I had nothing to do with that assault. Surely you don't think I could have?'

He was looking at Big Rose, and she was desperately trying to avoid his eyes.

Why did Jack want to believe him so much? A moment ago he'd thought him guilty of the most awful of crimes, yet he knew he didn't want him to be responsible.

The man was still watching his mother. 'Tell him, Rose. Tell him it couldn't have been me.'

She was watching him too, but finally she drew her gaze to Jack. 'He wouldn't do anything like that, Jack. Take my word for it.'

'Thanks, Rose,' the man said.

'I know you couldn't hurt anyone, Johnny. You couldn't change that much.'

Johnny. It was the first time he had heard her speak his name. Johnny. John was Jack's name. Jack was his nickname. She'd always told him he'd been called after his father. Somehow, he'd just never pictured his father like this.

Did she really believe him? She seemed to.

'He could charm the birds off the trees,' she had told him. Was that what he was doing now? Charming a bird called Rose?

The man looked at Jack, as if he had won him over. Did he think it would be that easy?

'Why should I believe you? I don't know you. Never did. And I don't want to.'

The man sighed and looked down at the floor. 'I'm going anyway,' he said.

Mum jumped from her chair. 'Going? Now? But the police will be watching the house.'

'I've been watching them too,' he said. 'They pass here every two hours, regular as clockwork. I'll be able to slip away in the middle of the night.'

Jack had never felt so relieved.

'Where will you go?' his mum asked.

'I'll make for the coast. Get a boat. I'll be OK.'

Jack watched him, tried to imagine him on the run. Standing there, in the glow of the lamps, he didn't look dangerous at all.

'I'll make you up some sandwiches.'

The man glanced at Jack, smiled. Jack had to force himself not to smile back. 'She thinks I'm going on a picnic,' he said.

Suddenly, a plate came flying across the kitchen and the man had to duck to miss it. 'I'm trying to help!' she yelled at him.

His voice was soft as he answered her. 'I know. I'm sorry. Don't let's quarrel. In the morning I'll be gone. You'll never see me again. I promise.'

'I hope so,' his mother said, bitterly.

Jack said nothing. He was glad the man would

be gone soon, yet in a strange way he felt sorry for him.

He wiped the pity out in an instant. Feel sorry for him? What was he thinking about. This man might be the monster who had assaulted a defenceless old lady. No! He wouldn't feel sorry for him.

'Thanks for letting me stay,' he went on softly. And thanks, Rose, for bringing Jack up so well. He's a son any father would be proud of.'

Then he turned and left the kitchen, closing the door softly behind him.

'There,' his mother said after a long silence. 'He'll be gone in the morning.'

But he wasn't.

Because by the morning all hell had broken loose.

24

*J*ack hadn't meant to sleep at all. He had planned to lie awake, listening for HIM going. But he had slept, and it was the phone ringing shrilly downstairs which had woken him. Jack checked his bedside clock – four-thirty in the morning. Who could be calling here at this hour?

He jumped from the bed and hurried downstairs. His mother was standing in the hall with the receiver clutched in her white-knuckled hand.

'What is it, Mum?'

Suddenly, HE appeared from the dark kitchen. He was ready to leave, his jacket buttoned up against the cold early-morning air.

'What?' he asked.

Jack's mother placed the receiver down, held on to it as if it was glued to her fingers.

'That was the local paper. Just to let me know the first edition is going to run the story of who Jack and I really are.' Now, she glared at the man, at Johnny, at his father, real hate in her eyes. 'They've found out! After everything I've done to hide it. They've found out.' She closed her eyes tight, as if she couldn't bear to think about it. 'It'll be on the front page. Happy now, Johnny? You've ruined your life. Now you're ruining ours.'

He took a step toward her. 'Rose, I'm sorry. I'll go now. It'll blow over.'

'It'll blow over?' she yelled. 'It'll never blow over for us. We're tarred for ever. A criminal's family. Your family.'

'Rose . . .' He moved closer to her. Suddenly, Jack ran, angry now too. Now that he could see his life changing for ever. It was bad enough when he'd had no father at all, when they'd called him 'Mummy's boy'. But now? What would they call him now, with his face and his mother's splashed all over the front pages?

He hated this man. Hated him. He pounded his fists against the man's chest. 'Why did you come here! I hate you.'

HE only stood with his hands hanging, doing nothing to stop Jack. It was his mother who finally pulled him away, pulled him close to her.

'You can't go now,' she said.

Jack turned on her. 'But, Mum –' he began.

'No, Jack. There's going to be a lot of attention paid to this house from now on. Reporters might be out there this very minute. No.' She shook her head. 'He'll just have to stay in the cellar until we can figure something out.'

Mum was right about the media attention. Less than an hour later there were reporters at the door. They camped on the grass at the front of the house, or sat in parked cars with cameras aimed at the windows. At about the same time the phone started ringing and didn't stop. There were so many calls they ended up unplugging the phone.

Jack couldn't even get to school. Not that he wanted to. The thought of facing everyone at school was what he dreaded the most. But what he also feared was that those reporters might find out who they had lurking in their cellar. If only they knew . . . could guess. HE was here. Right here under their very noses. What a story that would be.

Worse was to come in the afternoon.

The police arrived, clearing a way through the mass of reporters and stepping grimly inside the front door, filling the house with their presence.

Jack recognized the inspector. The one who had first spoken to mum.

'I'm sorry, Mrs Tarrant,' he said. 'I don't know how they found out. It certainly wasn't through us.'

Mum shrugged. She was pale and her hands were shaking a little. Other than that, Jack thought proudly, she was still the rock she had always been.

'I suppose it was bound to come out sometime,' she said. 'It's Jack I'm worried about.'

The inspector looked across at him. 'It'll soon die down, Jack. They'll go when they see there isn't a story here.'

Jack swallowed. How could they not read it in his eyes? There IS a story here – and it's down in our cellar.

The inspector only smiled. 'It's not very pleasant having all this attention, is it?'

Jack looked at his mum; couldn't find his voice. She spoke for him.

'No, it isn't. Couldn't you get them to go away?

We can't even get out of the house for them.'

'It might help if you make a short statement,' he replied. 'Just a few words asking them to understand your position. You haven't seen your husband for years, you've tried to protect your son. Ask them to respect your privacy.'

Mum hesitated. 'All right,' she agreed finally. 'And would there be any chance of a policeman being put outside?'

Jack gasped. Was she serious?

'Just for today, maybe,' she went on. 'Just to keep them away from the door at least. I know it's a lot to ask.'

'We're a bit understaffed, but –' the inspector smiled again – 'but we might manage one for the next couple of days. We'll make sure Jack gets to school too. How about that?'

She was the best, his mum, Jack decided then. She hadn't slept all night, she had Britain's Most Wanted hiding in her cellar, a horde of reporters on the lawn and a squad of policemen sitting in her living room . . . and here she was, calmly asking that one of them be left on duty outside the house.

No wonder, as they left the house, not one of those policemen suspected that she had the very man they were scouring the country for lying in a pull-down bed, not three metres below them.

25

*I*t was a policeman who took Jack to school the next day. No one knew he was a policeman, of course. He was in plain clothes and drove an old Ford Fiesta, but he was nice. He asked Jack all about school and football, trying to take his mind off his situation. Jack longed to yell at him, tell him the whole story. He had the power to make this nice policeman famous. Probably get him promoted. So why couldn't he open his mouth?

The policeman understood his silence, or thought he did. 'Don't worry about all those reporters. It's a nine-day wonder. They'll move on when they get a better story. They always do.'

At school, he was the centre of attention. Everyone was asking questions.

'Do you know where he is?'

'Why didn't you tell anybody?'

'You really never knew you had a father?'

His teachers rescued him from the questions, pulling him from the centre of a crowd whenever they could.

They couldn't be there all the time though. And today there was yet another rehearsal for the school show.

'Are you going?' Sandy asked. Sandy had surprised Jack. And pleased him. He pushed people away when their questions got too personal. He answered questions for him too. Usually by shouting. 'It's none of your blinking business!'

Jack saw that day he had a real friend in Sandy, not just a pal. He wished he could tell him everything.

'I might as well go, Sandy. I don't want to go home.'

'I don't blame you. Hey, maybe you could sleep over at my house.'

'That would be brilliant!' Jack said at once. Then he remembered his mum. He couldn't leave her there alone, with HIM. He had to go home.

Sandy understood. 'Just phone me if you need to talk.'

They arrived at rehearsals just as Angus Paige was going into his song. His costume, for the moment, consisted of a wig which kept falling off every time he tried to dance.

'He's rubbish!' Sandy whispered. 'You should be playing this part. You'd be dead good.'

'You're kidding,' Jack laughed. 'Do you not think I'm getting enough bad publicity.' They both laughed, attracting the attention of Lizzie who turned round and smirked.

'Oh, look who it is. Son of Hannibal Lecter.'

'Just ignore her, Jack,' Sandy advised him.

Jack tried, but it was hard.

'It must be nice at least to know you have got a daddy, even one as horrible as that.'

They began to move away, but Lizzie, thinking for once she had the upper hand, followed them.

'Now I know where you get your good looks from, Jack,' she taunted. 'From your daddy. I've seen him on television every night for the past week. Boy, is he ugly!'

Jack had had enough. He turned on her. 'You've got a cheek to talk. Even a plastic surgeon couldn't improve your fissog!'

'We'll have to stop calling you "Mummy's boy", and start calling you "Daddy's boy" instead. Like father, like son. You'll probably end up in jail as well.' She was yelling at him now and laughing. 'Daddy's boy! Daddy's boy!'

Jack was ready to fly at her. Sandy had to hold him back.

And then, suddenly, Joe was there, hearing the commotion – Lizzie's knight in an Adidas tracksuit. He didn't wait for an explanation. He assumed his lovely Lizzie couldn't be to blame. He just leapt on Jack, taking him completely by surprise, knocking him off his feet while the rest of the class gathered to watch. They rolled along the floor, trading punches that never seemed to hit their mark. Jack was just aware of Sandy taking bets on who could win. Joe seemed to be the favourite.

Then, they were both being dragged to their feet, still trying to claw at each other.

'That's enough, boys.' Mad Marshall held them by their collars. 'Both of you will be in the headmaster's office in the morning. I'm sick of all this fighting – and all over a girl.'

Over a girl? What girl? Jack was almost sick when he realized what girl he was talking about. Lizzie simpered and blushed.

Fighting over Lizzie Ferrier? Surely no one would believe that. And he'd thought today couldn't get any worse.

He was going home alone. If he had to run the gauntlet of reporters, it didn't seem to matter now. His mother would be waiting for him anyway.

Jack kicked a can out of the school gates and all the way up the street. Oblivious to everything but the thoughts jumbling inside his head.

He hardly heard the voice call him.

'Jack?'

He looked up. There was a woman standing by her car. She had blonde hair with black roots, and it looked as if it had been cut by someone who didn't like her. She smiled at him. 'Jack?' she said again.

He didn't acknowledge her, nor did he move toward her.

'Can I speak to you for a minute, Jack?' She took a step toward him and he moved back.

'I'm a friend,' she said.

Stupid thing to say. 'How can you be a friend? I don't even know you.'

'I should say . . . I'm a friend of your father.'

She had just said the wrong thing. 'I don't have a father.'

At least, she seemed to understand why he felt like that. 'I know. What a cruel way to find out. I'm so sorry. Look.' She fumbled in her bag and produced something from it. At first Jack thought it was a bus pass, but he moved closer and realized it was a Press badge.

She was a reporter. Emma Smith.

'Oh no!' He turned from her and would have run, but she held him back.

'Jack, I'm trying to help your father. I've been trying for years. I don't think he's guilty.'

He remembered him saying something about a reporter who was helping him. Jack turned back to her, intrigued, despite everything.

'I have new evidence, Jack. I'm sure now I have enough to re-open the case. If he would just come back.' She looked as if she really cared. 'If he contacts you, will you let me know, tell him. I think I could get him the pardon he's always wanted.'

He searched her eyes, very blue and clear. Did she know where his father was? Was she trying to trick him.

'I wanted to tell you, Jack, that I don't think your father is a criminal at all. I never have.'

He could charm the birds off the trees. Here was another of them.

She thought he was innocent? Well, his mum didn't. And if his mum thought he was guilty. Then so did he.

26

'At least the reporters have gone,' his mother said, peering through the blinds. She began buttoning her coat. 'Now, you will be OK, won't you?'

Jack still couldn't believe she was leaving him alone with HIM.

'I'm going to Mrs Ferriers,' she had said. 'She's been so nice, she's been in touch, genuinely worried about me, about us. Why don't you come? She asked us both.'

Jack hadn't told his mother about Lizzie's

taunts. She wouldn't think the family so nice if she knew about those. She'd be more likely to go over there and strangle Lizzie with her ponytail.

'Wish some of her niceness would rub off on her daughter,' was all he did say about the incident.

Big Rose smiled. 'I like her. She's not a wimp anyway. She can insult you as good as you can insult her.'

'Trust you to stick up for her,' he said. 'Anyway, I still don't see why you have to go. And leave me alone with HIM.'

'He's in the cellar, Jack. He won't come up now. It's too dangerous at the moment. And he'd never harm you. You must know that.'

Did he? Jack wasn't so sure. He hadn't yet told his mother about Emma Smith. He didn't want to talk about it at all.

His mother opened the door. 'I'm trying to make things appear as normal as possible, Jack. Going over to Mrs Ferriers, just for an hour, to see her.'

He looked out. It had begun to rain. 'Are you walking?'

'Of course. I'm going to suddenly produce a car from somewhere?'

He hesitated for a moment, reluctant to say what had been on his mind. 'I thought Alec might have taken you.'

They hadn't heard a word from Alec. Jack had

been disappointed. He had thought Alec was nicer than that. After all, he was almost his mother's boyfriend. Though, he realized since they'd had their unwelcome visitor in the cellar, the dates had stopped.

His mother, however, seemed to understand.

'I told him when I found out your dad was here that I couldn't see him any more. I made up some feeble excuse. He's been off on one of his courses, so I haven't seen him at work.' She sighed. 'Must have been a shock to him when he read the papers. He probably thinks I could have at least told him. He'll phone in his own time.'

She pecked Jack on the cheek. Thank goodness it was dark and no one could see her. Even the policeman had been taken off duty now that the reporters had gone.

Jack went back into the living room and slumped down on the couch. He almost jumped out of his skin when the phone began to ring. At first he was reluctant to answer it. They'd had so many weird calls since the news had broken, his mother had only just plugged the thing back in.

As it kept ringing, however, his curiosity got the better of him.

'Yes?' he asked cautiously, ready for a tirade of abuse.

'It's me, Sandy.'

He'd never felt so relieved.

'I forgot to remind you, what with all the excitement,' Sandy went on. 'That programme's on tonight.'

Jack was puzzled. 'What programme?'

'*Crime Scene*. Remember? The reconstruction. It'll be brilliant. Going to watch?'

Crime Scene. He had forgotten all about it. The old lady. The assault. Just about the time HE – down in the cellar – had arrived on the scene.

Of course he was going to watch.

Before he did, however, he tiptoed to the cellar door and listened. It was all quiet down there. Not a sound, not a breath. Jack turned the key in the lock. If there was going to be anything on *Crime Scene* to connect HIM with the assault, Jack would go to the police. He didn't care if he was grassing on his father. He didn't owe him anything.

And, if he was going to be alone in the house with a dangerous criminal, the dangerous criminal was going to be safely locked up. Exactly where Jack thought he should be anyway.

The local assault was the first crime dealt with on the programme. It was strange seeing streets he knew so well on television and people he recognized being interviewed.

The old lady was played by an actress, but all the other people involved were real. The local grocer told how he had sold the lady some cheese just before she began to walk home.

Halfway there it had begun to rain. Someone had seen her having trouble with her umbrella. And by the time she had arrived home, the rain had turned into a thunderstorm. People were sheltering in doorways to escape the deluge. Someone had seen a man in a doorway very near to where the old woman lived. All he could say was the man had his dark coat turned up at the collar. The police wanted this man to come forward so he could be eliminated from their enquiries.

Something buzzed in Jack's brain. He sat up.

In the police reconstruction it was clear that someone had forced themselves into the old woman's house as she opened the door. Had that someone been the man sheltering in the doorway? Had anyone seen a man acting suspiciously in the vicinity afterwards? He would have been hurrying from the scene. And there was a good chance his face would have been scratched or punched. The old woman had used her umbrella to good advantage and there were traces of blood on the handle.

Jack jumped to his feet. His heart began to pump. It all came back to him. The day of the thunderstorm, as he hurried home from school. He had decided to take the bus and had turned into a road not two streets away from where the old woman lived. He had bumped into a man with the beginnings of a black eye. He'd laughed, pointing out his own black eye. The man hadn't laughed back. He could see him now. Every detail of his unsmiling face, as close to his as it could possibly be.

He had seen him. He had seen him! It had all gone completely out of his mind because that was the same day he had seen his mother going into the police station.

Already on the screen they were listing the phone number to ring if you had any information. Then the number of their own local station.

Jack was off the couch in a flash. He had his hand on the phone when he suddenly stopped dead.

He couldn't phone the police. He had a wanted criminal hiding in the cellar. What if they sent a squad of officers to the house to interview him?

No. Jack couldn't take that risk.

He sat back on the arm of the couch thinking. He had to do something, but what? His heart was pounding with excitement, yet he felt his eyes drawn back to the television where the next reconstruction had already begun. Think, Jack! He kept telling himself. Should he phone Sandy? No, he decided. He couldn't risk getting anyone else involved. His mother? She could be at Mrs Ferrier's now. He could phone her, ask her advice. She would know what to do. He dismissed that idea almost immediately. She had enough on her mind and, anyway, he didn't want Lizzie Ferrier to know any of his business.

Crime Scene had just about finished when it suddenly struck him what he had to do.

He'd go to the station himself. His mum would crack up at him normally for leaving the house at this time of night, but she would understand this time. It was for a good cause.

He had seen that man so clearly. He couldn't believe it. Jack was excited and happy and . . . something else. It took him a moment to realize what that something else was. He was relieved.

The man in the cellar wasn't guilty of that horrible crime. He hadn't anything to do with it. His dad.

His dad. He stopped at the door thinking about that. It had been the first time he had thought about him that way. His dad.

Jack saw the future, bright and exciting. Jack would be a hero. The publicity from this would outshine the fact that he was a convict's son.

Things would get back to even better than normal.

YES!

He pulled open the front door and found his way was blocked.

Blocked by the man Jack had seen that day in the thunderstorm.

Jack gasped and took a step back.

'Aye aye,' the man said.

27

$\mathcal{J}$ ack took a step back, tried to shut the door, but the man's big hand pushed it open.

'Recognized me, did you?' His voice was low and gruff. 'Thought you might when you saw that programme.'

Jack was trying hard to speak. 'I . . . won't tell . . .'

'You won't? Where were you rushing off to then? The pictures?'

Jack couldn't think of an answer to that. In fact, Jack couldn't think at all. He took another step back. Such a mistake. The man was inside the house now, and closed the door behind him.

'I didn't know who you were either, till I saw your picture in the paper. Thought about you all day. I knew that face, but from where?' Now he had a horrible grin on his face. 'And then it struck me, you saw me that day. You and your black eye. And I had a feeling when you saw that programme you just might put two and two together. So I came over right away. I didn't have to watch the programme, you see. I knew who done it.' He had an ugly laugh.

'I'll not say a word.' Jack tried to sound convincing, though right at this moment he never meant anything so sincerely.

The man shook his head. 'No, you disappoint me. Here I find you rushing off to tell the cops as soon as the programme's finished.'

Jack had to do something. But what? 'I've already phoned the cops.' He blurted out, praying he would believe him. 'They're on their way now.'

Again he shook his head. 'You'd find that pretty hard, son, considering I've just cut your phone lines, and I've been here for a while. Saw your mother going. No policemen on the doorstep. Young lad in all by himself.'

Jack swallowed.

'You see, I've got it figured out,' the man continued. 'Anything bad happens to you they're going to assume it was your old man. Nasty bit of work he is. Found out where you lived and came and, well, they can figure the rest out for themselves.' He moved menacingly closer.

Jack could feel his heart pounding. He was in mortal danger here. He just knew it. Was he just going to stand there and take it?

No way!

Suddenly, Jack lifted his foot and kicked hard

against the man's shins. Caught by surprise the man let out a yell and clutched at his leg.

'You little . . . Come back here!'

But Jack was off, through the hall and into the kitchen.

He tugged at the back door. It was locked. He tried to struggle with the key, but he could hear the man behind him, hurrying closer.

Jack darted behind the kitchen door and held his breath.

The man rushed in, stopped for a second to look around for Jack.

Jack seized his chance. He gave him one almighty push and sent him reeling against the vegetable rack. Potatoes, leeks and onions cascaded everywhere, and when the man tried to find his feet he slithered all over the floor.

Jack was off again. Pulling the kitchen door tight shut, terrified, running for the front door. Even before he'd reached it he saw the key was missing. The man must have taken it. Jack turned and saw him race from the kitchen. Jack leapt for the stairs. Took them two at a time. Maybe if he could reach his room . . . there was a lock on his door. It might just stop the man long enough so Jack could make for the window, climb out, jump. Anything to get away from . . .

The man was almost on him. He could hear his heavy breath behind him on the stairs.

'I'm going to get you, son,' he yelled.

Not if I can help it, Jack thought.

He was at his room. He ran in and tried to push the door closed. But the man was already there, pushing against him with all his strength. Stronger than Jack, pushing and pushing, bit by bit widening the gap.

The man's fingers were curled round the door. With an almighty push Jack slammed the door against them.

The man screamed in pain, but it didn't stop him, only made him push harder.

If only someone would help him, Jack thought. And even in his terror he remembered his father, down in the cellar. Just below him. And he, Jack, had locked him in!

The man gave one final push and sent Jack flying on the floor.

He was standing over him. Jack couldn't move. He was too terrified to even think.

Suddenly, he could see no future for him at all . . .

28

'*T*ake your hands off my son!'

Suddenly, the man was pulled back, and Jack almost screamed with relief. His dad was there! He had the man by the shoulders, lifting him from Jack, pulling him round. He landed a punch against the man's face, who reeled back and almost fell on top of Jack. Jack rolled to the side and was on his feet in an instant.

'Phone the police. Get them here now!' His father ordered him. He was already on top of the man, holding him down.

Jack was watching, fascinated.

'Now, Jack!' His father yelled.

Jack raced for the stairs. All the while he was thinking. 'If I phone for the police they'll come . . . but they'll arrest my dad as well. My dad.' He thought the words for the first time with an affection he never thought he would have. His dad. His dad had risked everything to save him. His dad was willing to get sent back to prison for him.

His dad.

He was on the phone before he realized the

man had been lying. The line hadn't been cut after all.

'You could get away now,' Jack said to his dad as they sat on the stairs waiting for the police. The man was unconscious and bound in the room upstairs by this time. 'Before they come. I'll cover for you.'

He only shook his head. 'I'm tired of running. I've seen you ... and your mum. Maybe that's all I really needed.'

The police arrived before Big Rose came back. She was ashen white as she rushed in, not knowing what had happened. Jack was babbling out his story to some officers, while a strange man was being carried downstairs, his hands tied behind him with her beloved Gucci belt. And her husband was sitting on the stairs, handcuffed.

The inspector turned to look at her as she came in. 'We're going to need a statement from you too,' he said.

Jack stopped talking for a second and looked at her. He had never seen his mother so close to tears. The inspector saw it too. He patted her on the shoulders gently. 'Don't worry. Your husband's explained everything.'

Jack's terror had turned into nervous excitement. He found he just couldn't stop talking.

'Mum!' he ran to her, gabbling everything that had happened out in a few seconds. 'And Mum!'

He was pulling at her now, wanting her to take in the most important part of his story. 'He saved me!' He looked at his dad already being led from the house. He paused for a moment to look back at his son. Jack smiled at him. 'My dad saved me!'

'Will everyone get into their places!'

Mad Marshall was in his usual panic, even though the show was going extremely well. Granted, the caps for the guns hadn't arrived in time, so the cast still had to shout 'BANG!' every time they were fired, and the wheels of the Deadwood Stage had fallen off and landed on Bill Hickock. That really had made him Wild, and he had a fight with one of the cowboys. The headmaster had to break that up and give them a hundred lines each.

All this only seemed to make the audience enjoy it more and Jack and Sandy were having a ball.

'You looked brilliant in that frock, by the way,' Sandy told him. 'Did you hear everybody laughing?'

'It's the wiggle that does it!' Jack said, demonstrating.

Angus Paige had collapsed during the dress rehearsal. (Some unkind person said Mad Marshall had bribed him to do it.) And in true show business fashion, Jack as understudy had stepped in at the last moment and taken over the part.

'What made you change your mind?' Sandy asked him. 'About wearing a frock, I mean?'

'Because, Sandy,' Jack explained, 'a hero can wear anything he wants.'

And he was a hero. It had said so in the local paper. He had even been interviewed on television. The culprit was safely behind bars, thanks to him, and the old lady was on the road to a full recovery.

Well, thanks to him and his dad.

And his dad would soon be a free man.

The reporter, Emma Smith, hadn't been wrong about that new evidence. That and a deathbed confession by one of the other robbers had been the conclusive proof that his dad really had been framed all those years ago.

A programme on this particular miscarriage of justice had been shown just this week on television. His dad was getting a full pardon and would be out in only a few days.

Not quite home. Mum wasn't ready for that yet, she said. But he would be living and working in the town and building up a relationship with them both again.

For now, that was good enough for Jack.

He'd seen his mother in the audience with Mrs Ferrier and he'd never seen her so happy. Yes. That was good enough for Jack.

'Our mums seem to be enjoying the show, Jack.'

He turned to find Lizzie Ferrier grinning at him. She had grinned at him a lot, trying to be friendly. Of course, he was famous now, and a hero. It was worth her while to be friends with him. Jack didn't grin back.

'There's something different about you tonight, Lizzie,' he said looking at her closely. 'There's something missing.'

Suddenly, he realized that it was. 'Of course! Your spots. Come on. Lizzie, where are you hiding them?'

Lizzie's grin turned to a threatening frown. 'It's no use trying to be nice to some people,' she said. Then she sighed, very theatrically. 'What you don't seem to realize, Jack Tarrant, is that one day I'm going to be beautiful.'

Jack giggled. 'You wish.'

'While you, on the other hand, are always going to be stupid.'

'Are you calling me stupid?' He was getting annoyed at her now.

She sighed again. 'If the dunces cap fits . . . By the way,' she added with a smirk, 'loved you in the dress.'

'I look better than you in one anyway.' He said this a little too loudly. Joe Grady heard him.

He looked over, and his warpaint almost glowed. 'I've warned you before, Tarrant!' he shouted. And he leapt at Jack, waving his rubber tomahawk threateningly.

Suddenly, he was on top of Jack. Jack got a mouthful of Joe's feathered headdress and began to sneeze uncontrollably.

Mad Marshall rushed at them both. This was the last straw. He pulled them both, struggling, to their feet.

'You two boys, always fighting over this girl.'

And Jack stopped sneezing long enough to yell at the top of his voice, 'Will somebody please tell him I am not fighting over Lizzie Ferrier!'